MW01173687

ALICE AND THE BILLIONAIRE'S WONDERLAND

ONCE UPON A BILLIONAIRE, BOOK THREE

CATELYN MEADOWS

1

———

Maddox rested his hands on the edge of the rabbit enclosure and stared at the little furballs. In all the years he'd owned Wonderland, he'd never had much interaction with rabbits. Now, he stood before their display in Arbor Ranch and Supply, desperately hoping this last-straw idea of his would work.

It was hare-brained—no pun intended—but he couldn't lose the park. He had to do something. Sympathy wove through him as he took in the animals' gray, brown, and multi-colored furs. Stuck in their enclosure, no hope for escape without someone else's assistance.

"I get where you're coming from, guys," he told the rabbits.

"Tell me again why we're here?" his friend and associate, Duncan Hawthorne, asked from behind him. In suit pants and a tan button-up shirt with the sleeves rolled to his elbows, Duncan stared at the display of animal feed and various accessories with disdain. "I've never pegged you as much of an outdoorsman. Or a pet person, for that matter."

Maddox peered down at his own suit and tie. The irony

would have made him laugh if he didn't feel so downtrodden. Neither of them fit in with the store's rustic décor.

Duncan had come at Maddox's request, and he had it about right. This was the first time Maddox had ever set foot in a store offering western wear or livestock feed. He was more of a tennis player and golfer himself.

"Scavenger hunt," Maddox said. He'd given a lot of thought on how to increase interest in his declining theme park, and oddly enough, his mental deliberations had led him here of all places.

He couldn't let a rabbit loose in his theme park. Too many issues sprang up with that option. People might sneak their own white rabbit in and claim they'd found his. There also wasn't a way to humanely prevent the poor little creature from escaping the park, short of caging it, which would then make its location too obvious. And then there was the prospect of someone catching the rabbit at all, which was nearly impossible. On their own? With their bare hands?

A scavenger hunt throughout the park with a white rabbit at the finish line, though. That was totally doable.

"You're crazy," Duncan said. "Have you ever considered that the fact your numbers aren't where you want them to be is a sign you should just pack it in? Cut your losses, sell the place and move on to something that actually will be profitable?"

"Wonderland was profitable," Maddox argued. It'd made him a billionaire, after all. "I can't just walk away from the place. If I could just get some investors on board, I could do so much more with it."

Duncan read Maddox's not-so-subtle hint about wanting him to invest and lifted his hands. "I'm staying far away from that sinking ship. You opened a theme park in *Vermont*. You could have done it anywhere, but you picked Westville, Vermont."

True, the town was small, but that didn't mean it wasn't an ideal location for a theme park.

Maddox had appealed to his friend over a year ago, and many times since. But every time Duncan had asked for prospective numbers, what Maddox presented had never managed to impress him.

Several chicks in their nearby heated cages chirruped loudly. They were cute, too, if Maddox was interested in farming or free-range chickens. Which he wasn't.

"It's not a sinking ship." Maddox strolled to the opposite side of the rabbit enclosure. "People in Vermont like roller coasters as much as anywhere else. Besides, look. Here's a white one." He reached in to stroke it. The rabbit shuffled on the pen's shavings. "I wonder if we can have a little waistcoat made to fit him."

"You're going to dress the rabbit? Why not just get a Build-a-Bear?"

Maddox gave him a blank look. "Dude, have you even read *Alice in Wonderland*?"

"I don't need to read it. Everyone knows the story."

"Then you know Alice follows a rabbit wearing a waistcoat down his little hidey-hole, and that starts her whole adventure."

"I'll tell you what you need to do," Duncan said, clasping his hands behind his back and joining Maddox as he stared at the rabbits. "You've got good bones to the place. What it needs is a makeover. A new look."

"Wonderland doesn't need a new look." Maddox had used his mom's old sketches of her vision from the beloved story when doing the initial layout. He wasn't about to change a thing.

"Come on," Duncan said. "Everyone needs a makeover once in a while. Just spiff up the place. Add new signs, redo the décor. It might show certain *investors* you're serious about the future."

Duncan ran an extremely successful business where he offered financial advice as well as backing. Maddox had begged his friend to give Wonderland a chance and choose it as one of his investments. Was Duncan suggesting what he thought he was?

He held out a hand. "Hang on. You're saying if I give Wonderland a facelift, you'll consider backing it?"

Duncan tilted his head to one shoulder. "I might. The place does have some serious potential. To the right person."

Maddox had known him long enough to know he never even hinted at something unless he was serious. Empty promises were too risky when money was involved. For Duncan Hawthorne to even imply interest was a milestone.

Maddox gripped his shoulder. "You won't be disappointed."

"I haven't agreed to anything yet." Duncan shirked out of his grasp. "Why not start with a new brand? You find the right image to rep the park, and you might be turning *me* down."

Maddox laughed. He couldn't help the way his insides swelled like a hot air balloon. "Let me see how this rabbit stunt goes. It's a scavenger hunt, and I'm sure it's going to triple the numbers I usually get. I'm increasing publicity to spread the word. People are going to be all over this. Searching for the next clues to riddles? Finding the white rabbit at the end?"

"It is clever," Duncan said with an obliging nod.

"Come on, man, it's ingenious." Or so he hoped. He muscled down the worry tying knots inside him.

"Where'd you come up with it, anyway?" Duncan asked.

Maddox winced. If it was anyone else, he never would have confessed as much. But this was Duncan. They'd been best friends since freshman year at UVM.

"It was Ruby's idea," Maddox said.

Duncan's eyes widened. "Ruby, as in your ex?"

"Yeah."

"Are you seeing her again?"

The insulting question stung. It didn't help Maddox's surly

mood. "You're seriously asking me that? Come on, man. You know what she did to me."

Duncan knew just how much that breakup had rattled him. It was the sign of what a good friend he was, that he hadn't gone public with as much detail as he'd been privy to. With the amount Ruby had invested in Wonderland, calling their breakup messy was the understatement of ever.

Ruby had backed out of both their engagement and his business when profits had begun to sink. Evidently, she'd only been interested in him if his park was successful.

Her version of success was different from his. He had a billion-dollar theme park that reflected his mother's favorite book. He'd started it for her. It had made him a huge success and he couldn't lose it.

Lately, the park's appeal had all but vanished. The numbers weren't coming. In fact, with the cost of operating rides, maintenance, electricity, and staff, profits were drifting into the fiction category right along with the book it was based on.

Duncan's expression shifted from skeptical to apologetic. "Forget I said it. I just wanted to make sure this rabbit thing wasn't some ploy to get her back."

Maddox rammed away his uneasiness. Though his relationship with Ruby had ended badly, he did still hope to find someone to share his life with. But she would need to be someone he could trust, and Maddox wasn't sure someone like that existed.

He shook his head. "This is my livelihood. My mom's idea. I have to do this for her. I need investors."

"Whatever you say," Duncan said as a short, youthful associate with black hair and freckles made her way down the aisle toward them. "I'm going to go see if they have any turtles. There's a mock turtle in the book. Why not set one of those loose?"

"It's supposed to be a challenge," Maddox said with a laugh.

Duncan whirled to walk backward as he spoke. "Right. A challenge. Because everyone loves those."

"When I'm offering a cash prize big enough to feed a family for a year, they do," Maddox said as Duncan turned his back to him and strolled toward the display of saddles.

"Can I help you?" the cute associate interrupted. She wore an Arbor Ranch nametag on her plaid blue shirt, and cowgirl boots climbed up the ends of her jeans.

Maddox rubbed the back of his neck. Maybe he was crazy to do this.

He could tell the associate no thanks. He could leave the furry cottontails behind and find where Duncan had strolled off to. Or he could step out of the box and take a chance.

He'd always preferred that option.

"Yeah," he said. "I need a white rabbit."

This is going to work, he told himself as the associate assisted him with the rabbit. Whether the park was set in Vermont or not, he'd issue his challenge everywhere he could. Bring in new customers. He'd get Wonderland back on its feet.

All he needed was the right girl.

2

delie stared at the gigantic F-word on the top of the letter that'd just been hand-delivered by a balding sheriff.

Foreclosure.

Her mind spun, her thoughts turning to mush.

"This can't be happening," she said, closing her front door.

"Who was that?" Suzie asked, trotting over in her bunny slippers, with a steaming mug in one hand. Adelie couldn't form the words. Instead, she passed the notice to her sister.

Suzie's blonde hair was piled in messy perfection on top of her head. Her eyes skimmed the contents while a little line appeared between her brows. "How can this be? I thought we were caught up."

"We were." Adelie huffed and followed Suzie past the floral couches and into their farmhouse kitchen. The smell of sizzling hash browns and eggs filled the small room. They'd eaten hash browns and eggs for days. Thanks to their chickens that roamed the yard willy nilly, it was a cheap meal. "Until I lost my job. I've been so stressed trying to find work, but I thought you said you were going to take care of our mortgage payments until I found something."

"Right..." Suzie shifted, shuffling to place her mug on the kitchen's tiled counter. "About that."

Adelie blinked. "You haven't been paying the mortgage?"

Her sister was silly and spacey, that was true, but Adelie never thought Suzie would neglect something as important as this.

"I forgot I had to," Suzie said in a pleading tone. "All my money has been going toward school."

Adelie sank onto a chair at the kitchen table that had belonged to their grandparents. When Grandma and Grandpa Carroll both died—Grandma shortly passing after Grandpa had —Uncle Harper wanted to sell their house and get as much profit from it as he could. The girls hadn't wanted to sell it to anyone else. Having been raised by their Carroll grandparents, the two girls had grown up in this house. To think about selling the Sears-kit home with its back-in-time charm to anyone else had been unthinkable.

Instead of passing the home down to them, their uncle insisted on selling it to them. Fair enough, Adelie had supposed, since he had given them a decent deal on it. The sisters had thought they could swing a mortgage payment if they both did it together, but Adelie being unemployed, getting laid off from her position as a sales associate at Serendipity downtown, had lasted longer than she'd expected. She'd been job hunting, and prospects weren't looking good.

"What do we do?" Suzie said.

"We've got to make up the payments," Adelie said.

Suzie harrumphed and folded her arms. "How are we supposed to do that?"

They were surviving on fumes as it was. They'd already sold more of their grandparents' antiques and family heirlooms than they'd ever wanted to, but no matter what they did, the bills kept coming.

Adulting really stunk sometimes.

Medical expenses didn't help. Suzie had shoulder surgery over a year ago; it seemed like they'd be playing catch up for the rest of their lives.

Adelie peered around the beautiful, quaint kitchen, with its white cabinets and their smooth silver handles, at the buttercream wallpaper speckled with flowers, at the paneled window above the sink that unlatched in the center and opened without a screen, and at the exposed wood rafters in the ceiling above. Sure, it was cramped, but the house had too much charm to let it be foreclosed. Not to mention how this would ruin both of their credit. The idea sank into Adelie's chest like a rock.

"This is one of those times I wish Grandpa was around to talk to," Suzie said.

Same old Suzie. Always trying to help find solutions in any way she could. "Yeah, but he isn't. We've got to figure this out."

"We'll find somewhere else to live," Suzie said with a shrug.

The thought hurt. It was actually, *physically*, painful. "How could you say that so easily? You love this house as much as I do."

Unease sweltered in her empty stomach. She stirred the hash brown and egg mixture in the skillet and, as it was brown and yellow—murky, just like she felt—she turned off the heat.

The TV behind them blared and a news broadcaster piped up in their worried silence.

"What is Wonderland without a white rabbit? Pierre has gotten loose, and it's up to you to catch him. This is your chance to go down the rabbit hole and find the grand prize. Whoever follows the clues correctly and finds the white rabbit first gets a grand prize of fifty thousand dollars."

Reaching to dish a heaping helping of food onto their plates,

Adelie peered at the TV in the corner above their dishwasher. Cheers broke out in the newsroom on the screen. *Daylight News* anchors laughed and cheered, joking about this new opportunity.

The anchor in a fashionable suit, with her dark hair pulled back, faced the camera and continued. "Today, we have billionaire owner of Wonderland Theme Park, located in Westville, Vermont, Maddox Hatter, here to tell us more about it. So, Maddox, before we start, I have to know. Is your name a coincidence or a pseudonym you came up with when you started the theme park?"

Maddox crossed one leg to the opposite ankle and smiled. A heartbreaker kind of thing. Adelie bumped into the table and nearly dropped the plates in her hands. Attention equally plastered to the screen, Suzie apparently missed her sister's faux pas.

"Look at that," Suzie said. Adelie was curious about his reply, but with Suzie's interruption, she missed it. "It's a wonder she hasn't fainted yet."

Adelie sank onto the chair across from her sister. She couldn't deny her temperature had gone up a few notches. "Are you saying you would?"

"If I were in the same room with him, and he smiled at me like that? I'd be crazy not to."

"Crazy," Adelie mused, nudging her eggs with a fork and squirting some ketchup over the top. "This whole thing is crazy. Who gives fifty thousand dollars to some random person just for finding a white rabbit?"

If she had that kind of money, she'd want to use it to help others. She thought of her cousin, Ella's, fiancé. Hawk Danielson owned Ever After Sweet Shoppe, and this sounded like the kind of charitable thing he might do.

Suzie's voice cracked with excitement. "Are you kidding? This is the chance of a lifetime. Even if we didn't just get a visit from our friendly neighborhood police officer, we'd be mad not to jump at this."

Adelie swallowed and stilled. Her sister couldn't possibly be considering this. "Stop it right now. You don't actually want to go and try."

"Why not?"

Adelie pointed at the TV with her fork. "Do you know what kind of crowds are going to be there? He just broadcasted this on national TV. People are going to be traveling from far and wide for a chance at this."

To their cozy Westville. As far as towns went, it didn't get the massive traffic other big cities often did. It was a quaint little slice of heaven. They didn't need Disneyland-level tourism here.

"You know, the one I feel sorry for is that rabbit," said Adelie.

"Nah," Suzie contradicted her. "I feel sorry for all those poor suckers who'll be driving in from out of town. Because it's going to be for nothing. I'm finding that rabbit, Adelie."

"I don't think it's going to be that easy," Adelie argued.

"See these hands?" Suzie flared them in her direction. "Rabbit catchers."

Adelie laughed. "Good luck with that." She took another bite of buttery, ketchup-slathered hash browns.

"You sound like you're not coming."

Adelie finished chewing. "I'm not. I lost my job, Suz. I've got to find a new one, just in case your little plan to catch loose, four-legged creatures with cotton tails falls through."

"I thought Ella offered you a job," Suzie said with confusion.

"She's marrying Ever After Sweet Shoppe's owner, but that doesn't mean *she* owns the business. Besides, I don't want to accept her charity." Though the idea of working in a candy shop had been tantalizing. Her other grandma, Grammy Larsen, had discouraged Adelie from taking the position.

"You'd be great at it," Grammy had assured, "but being

around all that candy all day long? Makes my mouth water and my waistline expand just thinking about it."

Grammy had worked in one of the stores in downtown Westville for a year now, and she assured Adelie the part-time position wouldn't cover the expenses she and Suzie needed it to.

"You know you'd offer the same to Ella without a second thought if the situation was reversed," Suzie said.

That much was true. Adelie knew Suzie was referring to the surprise she and Suzie had helped their other grandma with last Christmas. Ella had been in need, though she'd refused to ask for any help. Grammy had gathered reinforcements to help clean Ella's apartment and convince her to attend the ball where she'd met her soon-to-be-husband.

But this was different. Adelie hated putting herself out there for anyone or anything. She preferred staying close to home, away from crowds. While she loved reaching out to help others, receiving help, on the other hand, or being around more than a handful of people at once, made her feel too exposed. She was the queen of reservation and caution, and she wasn't about to lose her crown.

"At least come to Wonderland with me." Suzie interrupted her musings.

Adelie shook her head. Suzie didn't understand. Her sister was an extrovert. Where crowds made Adelie want to cower in corners, they were like an IV pumping energy straight into Suzie's veins. She thrived off the attention and the vitality.

"Come on," Suzie whined. "This is our hometown. All these other people have to travel or drive long distances, but we're *right here.* You have to come. You've never even been to Wonderland."

"Because it costs a fortune to get in."

"It's one day," Suzie said. "It's a magical, whimsical, granted, campy, place, and how often do you get to see me rub elbows with thousands of others out to catch a rabbit? You know Fletcher can't go with me. He has to work. I *need* you."

Adelie could no longer hold down her smile. Suzie had always been good at melting her defenses. The Fletcher reference did the trick. Suzie's boyfriend was just as quirky as she was and would probably love something like this.

Suzie didn't usually beg, so Adelie knew this was something she *really* wanted. How could she tell her no?

It didn't completely alleviate the worry in her chest, but still, it managed to lift her spirits. "All right. I'll come—"

"Yay!"

"—but only to watch you make a fool of yourself."

"I'm finding that rabbit." Suzie punctuated the statement with a bite of eggs.

"I'll believe that when I see it."

Her sister smirked. "Then you have to be there to see it."

3

A delie exhaled through a part in her lips. This was worse than playing the lottery, something she'd never wanted to do because the chances of winning the jackpot were so unlikely it was laughable. Seeing these crowds? All these people who would use the same clues to find the same prize? They didn't stand a chance.

She couldn't help being charmed by the park's setup. The ticket booths sported top hat-shaped roofs. Towering rides, including a double-loop roller coaster, coiled through the sky above the park's fence. The sight gave Adelie a tiny thrill in her chest. She'd never ridden anything like that before.

The line trickled forward, and each step wound Adelie tighter with nerves. Just when she'd talked herself into accepting this scenario, they approached the window, and Adelie's mouth dropped.

Fifty dollars for the entry fee? That money was food on their table, and here they were, blowing it on some silly whim.

The woman behind the register, wearing a brightly colored, imaginative uniform with patched, puffy sleeves smiled patiently. Suzie, however, was the opposite of patient. She widened her eyes in a pointed sort of way at Adelie's hesitation, as if to say, *what are you waiting for?*

With a sigh, Adelie ignored her better judgment. She forked over the money from her wallet and received a ticket, a stamp on her hand, and a midnight-blue flier the size of an envelope.

"Your first clue is in here," the woman behind the register instructed. "You have until midnight tonight to find Mr. Missing Cottontail. Good luck."

"Thanks," Suzie said, beaming as she stepped through the silver, three-pronged rotation bar. Adelie followed, nabbing a park map from its distributive box in the process.

Suzie whirled around the instant they stepped out of the way of thronging people. "Let me see, let me see." She tried to tear the first clue from Adelie's hand, but Adelie yanked it to her chest and inspected the thick paper, then read the gold inscription aloud:

"It's rather curious, this sort of life."

"That's the clue?" Suzie said skeptically.

Adelie's brows furrowed. She'd read *Alice's Adventures in Wonderland* a long time ago, but she found herself intrigued by the quote, by the detail and depth someone had put into choosing it. A quote like that could be taken in multiple ways, which was probably what made it so appealing.

She couldn't allow that to give her false hope in this little scavenger hunt. She should be out job hunting. She should be doing something that could actually help them, not make them pilfer the little money they had left. A hundred dollars was a sliver she couldn't dig out.

"It can't be a clue," Adelie said. "I think it's just a teaser. Look, it opens."

"Here." Suzie reached for it again. This time, Adelie gave the card up willingly.

"They'd better be good riddles," Adelie said, examining the

milling crowd and the sheer number of people who'd stopped to read their cards just as she and Suzie had, "or this thing is going to be over within the hour."

Suzie didn't seem to have the same misgivings. She practically bounced on the balls of her feet. "Let's check them out."

She tore open the golden sticker in the shape of a top hat sealing the folded end of the blue cardstock.

It might have seemed less daunting if either of them had ever been to Wonderland Theme Park before. They'd grown up in this town, and while they'd driven past Wonderland countless times and seen the Ferris wheel and other rides tangling up the sky, Adelie had never once set foot here. She could have visited with school trips, but unlike Suzie, she'd always opted out of them. She was beginning to regret that decision.

Adelie leaned in to study the clue closer. Below a brief string of instructions, on the illustrated tag of the image's large glass bottle, were the words:

To begin, you'll have to start at the end.

Suzie lowered the paper in frustration and glanced around. People pointed excitedly toward a synthetic rabbit leaping toward a large, dark hole carved into the fake spread of grass. Others paused, taking selfies, rushing through what appeared to be a larger rabbit hole with a makeshift sign whose top plank was directed toward the hole.

"Start at the end?" Suzie said. "What does that mean?"

"Let's check the map." Adelie opened its folds, crinkling it and taking in the various attractions. The layout was extravagant and enticing, with bold, bright colors and easy-to-follow routes to get to every ride.

"What are you looking for?"

"In the book, they play croquet at the end. Does this place have anything like that? Oh, look." She pointed to a large flamingo marking an attraction called *The Queen's Croquet-Ground.* "Let's start there."

Linking arms, the sisters wove through the crowds for what felt like miles until they made their way to a large ride set off by a flamingo next to a hedgehog. Playing cards with heads, arms, and legs were situated here and there, as well as a sign. On it, a cartoonish depiction of Alice scolded a disobedient flamingo.

"Do we ride the ride?" Suzie asked.

Adelie took in the whirling carriages shaped like fat hedgehogs. The hedgehog carriages spun and dodged in and out of sight along a track. A trail of people so long it interrupted traffic coiled along. "I don't think so. Look how long that line is." Besides, they weren't here to ride anything. They needed to find that rabbit and vamoose.

Adelie searched their riddle, skimming the instructions they probably should have read before they started. Skim...skim... there. "*For clues that lead to rides, the next clue will only be given after your enjoyment of that particular attraction.*"

Her dismay deepened. "Never mind. Looks like that's a yes, we do need to ride it."

"Come on." Excitedly, Suzie tugged Adelie over to the end of the ride's line.

The sisters indulged in ride after ride and received clue after clue. Adelie had to admit, she would have loved to come any other time, if money wasn't so tight. If she didn't feel like every ride, every line, every step toward the next clue and the next—clues that hundreds of others had already found—made things seem that much more hopeless.

~

Maddox paced the park. He couldn't help checking the camera feeds from his phone, to see if the final riddle had been solved yet, but so far, no one had discovered the rabbit he'd named Pierre.

He could have watched from the sidelines, but that was no fun. Instead, he'd opted for meandering and soaking in the energy that had tripled at every turn. This was what Wonderland was meant to be about. The fun. The marvel, the discovery, the pure enjoyment. Maddox breathed it all in like a drug.

Around lunchtime, he stopped into the Ever After Sweet Shoppe for a fruit smoothie—peach mango, his favorite—and a toasted turkey and cranberry panini. He'd suggested the *Sweet Shoppe* in the park offer more than just candies and goodies, and it had turned out to be a good idea.

As he sat eating near the window, a pair of women caught his eye. Or rather, one woman. Of all the people he'd been watching today, with their gaping smiles and easy laughter, this woman was not only beautiful, but also apparently grumpy.

"Not the reaction I'm going for," he muttered to himself with a smile, taking a final sip from his smoothie to finish its contents. It wasn't her apparent displeasure alone, though. His gaze was drawn to her. She had a spark about her, from her creamy pale skin that matched the color of her hair to the cautious way she approached the *Odds N' Ends* gift shop. Something told him she was that way about everything. Cautious. Careful. And completely oblivious to the effect she had on others around her.

Driven by a force he couldn't explain, he hurried to toss his sandwich wrappings and empty cup in the garbage and made his way out.

Odds N' Ends was Maddox's favorite shop in the park. It offered the widest variety of souvenirs and do-dads for tourists. The shoppers were charmed by the shelves offering teacups and tiny bottles of liquid, by the white kid gloves, the stuffed cats and mice and flamingos, the croquet sets made up of flamingos and hedgehogs. Maddox's best-selling item was a T-shirt saying *Curiouser and Curiouser* on one side while the back declared, *I forgot how to speak good English at Wonderland,* above the Wonderland Theme Park logo.

This time, though, the merchandise, the associates, the displays, it all blurred. Even through the packed crowd of shoppers, he saw only her.

The woman stood before a Victorian display featuring lace doilies on antique suitcases surrounding a lamp dripping with fringe on its shade. She lifted a finger to tap one of the beads dangling from the lamp shade's fringe. Wonder filled her gaze, and Maddox's heart seized in his chest.

"Alice," he breathed, taken by astonishment. "That's her. She looks just like her."

He couldn't let this woman out of his sight. He had to talk to her. Not paying attention, Maddox kicked the edge of a display table covered with teacups staggered on separate stands. The entire display trembled, the china tinkling. Heat flamed in his cheeks. Patrons glanced in his direction. Maddox waved to them and then righted himself, only to knock down a decorative, black teapot that sat too close to the table's edge. He lunged for it, but too late, the teapot shattered on the floor.

People nearby gaped at him. Great. That was just what he needed—for anyone who might recognize him to see the park's owner making a fool of himself. Hurriedly, he spun around and signaled for the nearest employee.

"Sorry about this, Clark," he said, reading the young man's nametag. He couldn't possibly know everyone who worked for him. "This was my fault. Can you get that cleaned up?"

"I—sure..." Clark said, but Maddox didn't stay to finish their conversation. Quickly, he scoured the shop for a sign of what rabbit hole the woman—the perfect Alice—had disappeared down, but his heart dropped. The shop's bell tinkled, and in a flash of blonde hair, she was gone.

"I'm starting to think there is no rabbit," Adelie overheard one frustrated patron mutter to another as she took a stuffed rabbit to the nearest cash register.

Adelie had to say she agreed with the woman. She and Suzie had been here for hours and still had barely managed to find the fourth clue. "How many clues were there?" she wondered aloud.

She'd paused to admire a charming lamp with dripping beads along its shade when the sound of crashing porcelain startled her. People had clustered near the scene of the crime. Adelie spotted Suzie immediately and ushered her toward the exit. The last thing they needed was for the employees to think either of them had been the culprit for the crash.

Out in the sun once more, she could see many patrons still examining their clues. Others, however, seemed to be enjoying themselves, not caring about the prize at all—pushing strollers, buying treats for their children, and laughing in the spring sunlight.

"Tell me again what the next one said," Suzie said as she ambled along beside Adelie. She'd stopped to inspect and admire a squat building labeled *The Duchess's House*. A cross-looking woman holding a baby could be seen through the window, and the Cheshire Cat smiled and blinked in and out of view from behind a tree.

It didn't matter what others said, Adelie had always thought he was creepy.

She pulled up the last clue they'd gotten after the *Pool of Tears*. The water ride's inflatable boats carried them over rapids and around treacherous rocks, surrounded by mice and birds. Her shoes and shirt were still wet, and the chilly March air didn't help. The snow had melted mostly everywhere, but it was still cold.

"*Why is a raven like a writing desk?*" she repeated. "Ugh, this is maddening. Even Lewis Carroll said there was no answer to that riddle. How are we supposed to find one?"

"Don't you love that we share a last name with him?" Despite her pronouncement to find the rabbit, Suzie seemed oblivious that they'd made absolutely no progress.

"It's not his real last name," Adelie said, exasperated, trying to think things through, to see where others might be heading. If they didn't at least try, this whole day would all have been for nothing.

"What if it's not in reference to a ride this time?" Suzie suggested.

"What do you mean? They've all referred to rides."

"You've read the book," Suzie said. "What does that line have to do with anything?"

Adelie considered her sister's question. The instruction on their pamphlet did imply not every clue would lead to a ride. If not a ride, then where?

"In the book, the riddle is said by just another crazy character while Alice is having tea at the March Hare's house."

"Then we go to the March Hare's house." Suzie declared this as if this was the simplest thing in the world.

Adelie pulled up the map. "You know, that's not a bad idea." Too bad everyone else who'd already gotten the clue was probably there too. Whoever had thought this whole scheme up needed to be shaken.

"It's this way," Adelie said as the mechanized Cheshire Cat reappeared from behind his tree and rolled his eyes at her.

Holding hands to stay together through the thick masses, the two sisters passed a robotic man dressed in a caterpillar suit on a large mushroom, holding a hookah and shouting out dizzy commands.

"The rabbit will be released at half-past ten. You'll have the day to find him, though you'll need more than time if you want to catch him. You'll never catch him. I never said you would."

People moseyed along, some stopping to admire a large waterfall. Others gathered at kiosks for breadsticks or corn on the cob. Workers swept the pave stones, collecting bits of garbage and fallen popcorn.

A thickset, cartoonish house came into view. Its thatched roof was interrupted by pointed bunny ears sticking straight up out of the rooftop. A sign with a caricature Alice holding a teacup labeled it, "*March Hare's Mad House. Keep your wits about you.*"

Throngs milled, stepping into the oddly shaped front doors and into apparent darkness beyond. Brief spurts and short shrieks of laughter escaped with each entry. Inwardly, Adelie dug in her heels. Whatever was going on in there, she wanted no part in it. Someone had to be the spoilsport. Might as well be her.

She pivoted, taking in the long, curved, fiberglass table situated in the March Hare's front yard behind a low, white fence. The table was bright blue, its sides striped like a barbershop pole. Teacups of every size and shape littered the curved surface, and a mechanical dormouse appeared to reside in the center-most mug, popping in and out with crazy eyes and spouting out, "Twinkle, twinkle little rat."

"It doesn't look like a ride," Adelie said suspiciously.

"Maybe it's not one," Suzie replied. "Maybe it's a walk-through and we'll find the rabbit inside."

Another cutesy sign, which gathered giant, fiberglass mush-rooms at its base, read, *Stuff and Nonsense. Don't believe anything you see within. If you get lost, just wait a while. The way out will come back to you.*

"Sounds promising," Suzie said. "It's like a funhouse."

It sounded like anything but fun. Had whoever crafted this hunt put the rabbit in there? Was that why no one had found it yet? She glanced around, settling on a decision. This would be their last stop. If they didn't find the rabbit in there, they weren't going to find it anywhere.

4

"Poor bunny," Adelie said. "It's probably scared to death being hunted by all these people."

"It's a rabbit. It doesn't care." Suzie stepped onto the cartoonish path toward the door and paused to peer back. "You coming in?"

There was no point. With all these people? The weird clues? This entire situation was a ploy. Like the lottery, the likelihood of winning, of finding this supposed rabbit, were slim to none.

"Not a chance," Adelie said. "Knowing my luck, I'll be the one getting lost, and you'll have no riddles to help you find me." She added a smile to lighten the statement. "I'm staying right out here, where I can breathe. And Suz, after this, I'm going home."

Suzie's face fell. She broached the few steps back to Adelie's side. "I thought you were having fun with me."

A hint of remorse struck her. Suzie had always been flighty and daring, while Adelie was the timid, down-to-earth type determined to keep her feet on the ground. She should have known not to leave paying the mortgage in her dreamy sister's hands. It was almost like she was a child instead of a few years older than Adelie's twenty-five.

Adelie gave her a smile, trying to will away the skepticism that had been plaguing her since they arrived. She hoped it was enough to make up for her surliness. "It's not that. This has been really fun, probably the most fun I've had in a long time."

"Then why can't you just loosen up?" Suzie shook Adelie's hand by the wrist.

Adelie dipped her head. "I'm sorry, I wish I could. I'm just worried, Suz. Guilt has been eating at me since we got here. I can't spend the whole day here when I could have been looking up places that accept washouts who can't find work anywhere else." Another smile. At this point, she'd have to start applying at fast food places.

She was really looking forward to getting her nursing degree, but until she finished school, she'd have to do what she could to make it through. Adelie wished she could skirt around her worries and indulge in the lighthearted fun everyone else around her seemed to be having. But she'd been born practical, it was in her nature. And her practicality couldn't allow her to ignore the threat hanging over her head with every step she took.

"All right then," Suzie said, shaking her head as if dusting away Adelie's doldrums. "But you're so missing out. See you on the other side."

Adelie laughed and waved to her sister as Suzie stepped through the door. Several more people quickly entered behind her.

Pivoting, Adelie shuffled the few feet and took one of the empty seats around the vacant tea table. Her feet aching, her soul weary, she rested her elbow beside a plastic triangle of cheese, plunked her head into her hand, and began tracing the rim of a wide, pink polka dot teacup with her finger.

She should have lied. Told Suzie how awesome the day had

been, pretended away her worries. That had never been her style, though. She was honest to a fault, and timid as well.

If it hadn't been for Suzie, she probably wouldn't have done half of the gutsy things she'd attempted in her life. Like trying out for the community softball team. Volunteering on the community theater board to direct teenagers on the light and sound crew. Signing her name on the mortgage of their late grandparents' house.

She released a sigh with that last thought. What were they going to do?

"You look lost."

A man leaned his hip against the table. If the blue, striped teacup hadn't been fiberglass and attached to the cutesy table, he would have tipped it over and spilled its contents.

He may as well have tipped her over though. The insides of her brain were slowly seeping out. His mahogany hair was gelled away from his forehead, his green eyes held teasing glints of riddles and rhyme, and he rested a hand on the table as he stared. Right. At. Her.

Her heart picked up the pace. He looked familiar. Why? Where had she seen him before?

She shook herself, remembering too late to reply. "No, I'm not lost. I know exactly where I am."

"And where is that?"

She raised her brows, glancing around. Could anyone be here and not know where they were? "Do I really have to answer?"

He sank onto the orange, backless stool beside her. She caught a whiff of his warm, amber musk. "No, you don't *have* to. But if you did answer, what would you say?"

He was too gorgeous for his own good. How could anyone be that good-looking? Adelie found herself tongue-tied, unable to form a coherent answer. Something about his tousled hair, the mischief dancing in his eyes, and the seduction in his smile made her feel like a pot set to boil. Her temperature rose. Bubbles reached the surface, and heat coursed through her the longer he sat there staring at her.

"I'm in Wonderland," she said. "At a mad tea party while thousands of people are chasing a white rabbit."

"No rabbit-chasing for you?"

She grinned in a sardonic kind of way, attempting to slow her racing pulse. "I'm not that desperate."

Well, she kind of was. But she wasn't about to admit it to *him*.

He rested an arm on the table. "What would make you be?"

Adelie was taken aback. She wasn't sure she'd heard him correctly. "What would make me be desperate?" That was an odd question for a first meeting. Not to mention kind of personal.

He shrugged. "Desperate enough to put it all on the line for a silly white rabbit chase?"

She couldn't follow his train of thought. Who asked questions like this? Still, this flirting was harmless. She'd be off and leaving the park as soon as Suzie came back out again.

Adelie rotated on her stool and decided to humor him, though the directness of his gaze didn't help her pulse. "If I were going to be desperate, it would have to be over something I really wanted. Something that meant more to me than anything else in the entire world."

"And that might be?"

Adelie rubbed her hands together and stared off at nothing for a moment. "Security," she said unexpectedly. "Knowing everything is going to be okay."

He considered her answer for a moment. "Sounds worth it," he said, his voice deep.

She couldn't believe she'd opened up to a practical stranger.

Adelie needed a subject change, stat. "What about you? You're not interested in finding the rabbit?"

"Don't worry. I'll get what I wanted out of this," he said, winking at her before standing up and striding away.

Adelie stared after him. Their exchange played over and over again with every step he took. Without a doubt, that was the weirdest conversation she'd ever had with a total stranger. Catch the white rabbit? Please. Chasing rabbits led Alice into a totally bizarre world that she couldn't escape from until she woke to find it was a dream.

Adelie didn't need the distraction of dreams. She needed reality; a new job, to make enough to catch up on their mortgage, and to keep her feet firmly on the ground.

People were visible through the windows of the fun house. They treaded in and out, flocking in a steady line to and from the front of the park. Looking beyond, Adelie allowed herself to be momentarily hypnotized by the whirling rides and the distant, lazy Ferris wheel.

"Why is a raven like a writing desk?" she muttered, bumping her elbow into the plate beside her.

The table hummed beneath her. The plate began to sink. A creaking noise sounded. The mechanical dormouse in the center of the table stopped his repetitive mutterings and descended slowly into the table itself. Cups disappeared, and in the middle of the transformation, as the table lost part of its contents, a cage slowly began to rise in their place at the table's center.

"What in the—?" Adelie couldn't finish.

Inside the cage before her, a fluffy, white rabbit wearing a red and blue-striped waistcoat sat and wiggled its nose. Its long ears went straight back on alert, and it stared at her with wary, red eyes.

"No way," Adelie said to herself, pushing to her feet and

staring at the transformation. Had she made that happen? She glanced around just to be sure.

"Look," someone shouted. "Look at that!"

"She did it. That girl—see that lady? She found him."

"She found the white rabbit!"

Noise exploded. Applause signaled behind her. People gathered faster than kids to an ice cream truck. The handsome, strange man appeared at her side, clapping along with everyone else. The expression on his face was different though. Intuitive. Almost proud, though she wasn't sure how that could be.

She lifted her hands in surrender and attempted to step back, losing her footing against the stool she'd been sitting on. "I —I didn't know it would do that; I swear."

"Something always happens here when those words are spoken," the man said, sidling close to her and leaning in to be heard over the crowd, which had doubled in size in minutes. "But not many guests know it. I've kept it a secret on purpose."

"You—you kept it secret?"

"Congratulations," he said, flashing a knee-knocking smile at her. "You've won the scavenger hunt."

The crowd clustered around her. People shouted and whooped exclamations of surprise and amazement.

Adelie's mouth gaped. Her pulse pounded as the roaring noise around her increased to a deafening din. The good-looking man removed a phone from his pocket and spoke into it with one finger in his left ear, waving over what appeared to be a news crew.

The ground turned to glue. Adelie glanced around in desperation. Where was Suzie? Had she made it out of the fun house? She was the one who wanted to find the rabbit, not Adelie. What was she supposed to do now?

"You look a little shocked," the man said, putting his arm around her and guiding her away from the tea party table and to the open path between the park's street and the March Hare's house. "You've just won my contest's grand prize."

He handed a letter to her, one in the same midnight-blue cardstock with the now-familiar same gold writing swirling across it. Another quote from the book probably, but Adelie couldn't bring herself to concentrate enough to read it.

"You—*your* contest?" She took the folded letter he offered and held it in her hand.

"Sure," he said. "This is my park. And you've just won my challenge. You've just won fifty-thousand dollars."

Adelie couldn't think. She couldn't believe it. She'd found the rabbit. And the man who'd been sitting at the table with her? Had been Maddox Hatter.

5

A delie's brain had turned to cotton. Cameras flashed. Phones took the place of faces. The rabbit skittered in its cage, and someone pronouncing herself as Wendy Hendricks kept ramming a microphone in Adelie's face and asking for her name.

"A-Adelie," she managed.

"Got a last name, Adelie?" Wendy asked, tipping the mic to her. A man in a blue baseball cap appeared, cradling a large, black video camera labeled WV3 on his shoulder and directing it right at her. Was she being recorded?

"Carroll."

Crowds filtered out from the March Hare's house, squeezing in as tightly around the area as they could. Maddox waved to them in greeting as though completely thrilled that even more people were attempting to squish into a space that was already packed. Someone else—a woman—barked an announcement over the crowd, shouting her name over and over.

"Adelie Carroll is the winner. Adelie! Adelie Carroll!"

Some clapped. Some folded their arms in disgust. Some shot glares so piercing they might as well have been daggers. Suzie mustered through the crowd, pushing past everyone with a fervent declaration.

"Excuse me, that's my *sister!*"

Relief stole over Adelie like a downpour. Suddenly, things were a little easier with her sister there. Suzie gripped her hands and bounced up and down, squealing with delight. She kept repeating the same words over and over before moving on to the next.

"You? You. Did it. You did it!"

Adelie tucked a hair behind her ear. Suzie's excitement was doing the job, trickling in and injecting her with its own dose of disbelief. This morning, she'd been despondent, frustrated and borderline hopeless. She never in her wildest dreams could have imagined this.

Fifty-thousand dollars for finding a bunny in a cage?

"All this for a scavenger hunt?" she mused, but the crowd around her was so deafening, she could barely hear herself.

"It is hard to believe," Wendy went on, signaling to quiet the crowd. "When you came here this morning, did you ever think you'd actually win such a grandiose prize?"

"No," Adelie said, warming up to the newscaster. A smile crept onto her cheeks. "I never thought I would."

"Mr. Hatter," Wendy turned to Maddox. Adelie had forgotten he was standing beside her. "Did the challenge take as long as you anticipated?"

"Not at all," he said. "I thought it would be something swift. The clues weren't all that challenging, at least not enough to be impossible." He smiled. "I knew the table would be the trick."

"So, tell me, Adelie," Wendy said. "How exactly did you get the rabbit to appear?"

Adelie tried to think back to what had happened. She'd said the riddle aloud; it had served as a verbal password, triggering a chance she never expected. Who knew the table would respond to a code like that? It made her wonder what Mr. Hatter usually kept in there.

"I—I just spoke the riddle to the table," she said.

Wendy's forehead indicated her confusion.

Mr. Hatter stepped in. "It's always been something, one of those hidden tricks I never informed people about. A few have discovered it here and there, but anyone who sits and says those exact words, where the trigger can catch them, unlocks the table."

Wendy's mouth gaped open. She appeared completely spellbound by his words. Or maybe it was just standing close to someone who looked like he did. His eyes had the effect of a magnet.

"Incredible." She shook herself before turning back to Adelie. "Tell me, Ms. Carroll. What are you going to do with your winnings?"

Adelie hesitated. She wasn't sure where this interview would be broadcasted, and she wasn't about to tell the entire world her problems or about the foreclosure with her house.

"I'll figure something out," she hedged with a smile. At this point, she could no longer manage to clear it from her cheeks, and if she was being honest, she didn't want to. Fifty-thousand dollars. She'd won fifty-*thousand* dollars.

Wendy turned to the cameraman to give her take on the report, and Mr. Hatter tilted in. "First interview?"

Adelie stared around the park in wonder as if seeing it for the first time. The lightness she'd longed to feel was there now, giving her the impression she was floating. Exhilaration fluttered through her, spiking her adrenaline in a way she hadn't felt in a long time.

"First everything," she admitted.

Another man with blonde hair and a zip-up jacket joined Mr. Hatter's side. He punched him in the shoulder and inclined his head to his left. Mr. Hatter nodded to him in unspoken communication and then tilted in again.

"Excuse me, Miss Carroll. Now that the surprise is over, I think we should take this to a quieter location. Would you care to join me?"

Oh goodness, this was really happening. She was really his grand prize winner. Adelie wasn't sure what was more spine-tingling: that she was the winner, or his proximity and the prospect of having been invited somewhere by him. Either way, she'd take it.

Get a grip, she told herself. *He's only inviting you because you're his winner.*

"Where?" she managed.

"My office. Things will be much calmer there, and I can answer whatever questions you might have."

Questions. Yes. She had those. Adelie had to admit, after such a bustling, emotional day, some solitude would be nice. She'd been looking forward to escaping the noise and crowds.

"That would be great. Do you mind if my sister comes?"

"Not at all."

Mr. Hatter waved to the crowd, but it was already dispersing. People weren't leaving the park, though—they were riding rides and enjoying their day in spite of the contest's close. Several park guests even commended him on such a fun idea.

Dozens of riddle cards littered the walkways, being picked up by workers in imaginative, baggy uniforms with brightly colored pants in varying shades of the primary colors. Adelie walked in an unbalanced way as if on loose ground, her brain disconnected from the rest of her.

Suzie linked arms with her, slanting in as they went. "You!" she said under her breath. "You said you didn't even want to come, and now look what happened."

"I know. I know." Adelie picked up the pace, scurrying to

keep up with Mr. Hatter and his friend. The two men were caught in conversation, speaking in hushed tones a pace in front of them, darting the occasional glance back at Adelie. Every time his gaze connected with hers, it cinched something in her stomach.

What were they saying? Were they talking about her? If so, she wasn't sure how she felt about all this attention.

"What's the scoop?" Suzie asked under her breath. "When do you get the money?"

Adelie shushed her. Mr. Hatter said he would tell her. She wasn't about to be greedy about it or demand the money. This was his offer, his challenge, and he would make good on it, considering the crowds and the news crew that still seemed to be flocking, filming rides and interviewing participants. Wendy and her cameraman lingered near the mechanical caterpillar on his mushroom with another group of people who claimed they'd seen the whole thing happen.

Mr. Hatter and his friend stopped before a house with the words *W. Rabbit* on the nameplate in the grass out front. It had a thatched roof like the March Hare's house, kitschy but without the ears.

"In here," Mr. Hatter said, leading the way around the back. He ambled along a series of steppingstones veering to a misshapen door with a fat knob and a tiny keyhole. Mr. Hatter rested his thumb on a portion of the windowsill. A beep sounded, a small green light flashed, and he turned the too-big knob to enter.

Adelie and Suzie exchanged a look. She would never have guessed the door would open at all, let alone lead into what appeared to be the back end of a prestigious office.

The interior was completely different from the park's exaggerated details. This was plain and stuffy, devoid of pictures on the walls or anything to add contrast apart from speckled linoleum beneath their feet and the blinds covering the windows.

"My office is just through here," Mr. Hatter said. He slowed his pace to match Adelie and Suzie's and led the way down the short hall. Where did this lead out to? She wished she'd paid more attention to the house's surroundings.

"Did you ladies enjoy your time at the park today?" he asked.

"Are you kidding?" Suzie responded. "It was amazing. The rides, the crowd, the rush. Seriously, we've had the best day."

Mr. Hatter smiled at her as they rounded a corner, but his eyes moved toward Adelie. She was used to Suzie soaking up attention from men. It'd been that way for as long as she could remember. And though Suzie had a great boyfriend right now, Mr. Hatter wouldn't know as much.

At this point, when they'd meet men the first time, most guys would keep their attention on Suzie for the remainder of the conversation. Not Mr. Hatter. His interest deepened as it landed on Adelie. She couldn't help but sizzle under the impact.

"And you, my winner? What did you think?"

His winner. She'd never been a man's anything. Adelie chided herself. She really needed to stop acting as though he had any interest in her aside from being a participant, and winner, today.

Multiple answers strung through Adelie's mind. She settled on the least confusing one. "I think everything was unexpected."

"Unexpected?" His brows lifted. "That's a substantial word."

Substantial? Adelie thought it over. That could be taken in a few different ways, she supposed. She decided to clear whatever confusion he had.

"I meant it in a good way," she said. Too good. The words *fifty-thousand dollars* continued to trumpet in her mind.

They turned another corner and approached a receptionist sitting at the desk. She gave them an acknowledging nod. Mr.

Hatter tapped the desk in greeting before leading the way to an office.

The space was bright, professional, and squared. Squared room, squared-off black, leather chairs, even the pots holding plants along the window were square. Still, it was comfortable, as much as an office could be.

"Please, have a seat," he said, gesturing to a pair of armless, leather chairs.

Suzie took the farthest one with so much exuberance it slid from its place on the floor. "Whoops," she said sheepishly, scooting it back into place.

Adelie sank into the seat next to her. Mr. Hatter sat in his seat and the other man, in jeans and a button-up shirt beneath a zipped-up jacket, rested his weight against the bar off to the side.

"This is my associate, Duncan Hawthorne," Mr. Hatter said.

Mr. Hawthorne gave a small wave.

"I want to formally congratulate you, Miss Carroll," Mr. Hatter said.

Away from the crowds and the pressure of the moment, the pieces began to click together. Her breathing came easier, and her thoughts seemed to be less scrambled. "That's why you were there at the tea table," Adelie said. "You were waiting for someone to figure it out."

"I'd been wandering around March Hare's house all day," he said.

"So?" Suzie piped in, her eyes darting from one man to the other. "Fifty-thousand dollars?"

6

"Suz." Adelie dipped her head in embarrassment. Her sister had many childlike qualities, but this lack of filter —or apparent lack of any tact whatsoever—left something to be desired.

Mr. Hatter chuckled and stood from his seat, coming around to slump against the front of his desk. "Yes. About that. How would you feel about a different offer, Miss—can I call you Adelie?"

"Sure," Adelie said, fighting the sinking in her chest. "And what do you mean, a different offer?"

He slid a look to Mr. Hawthorne, who inclined his head with insistence.

"Wonderland's brand is ready for a new look," Mr. Hatter said. "And I think it's you."

"What's me?"

"For the rebrand. New logo. New signs for every ride. New brochures, new maps. I need a girl to be the face for that. It's you. I need you to be my Alice."

"Your—Alice?"

Suzie's feet drummed on the carpet.

Adelie's brows crunched. "Why? I mean, why me?"

"I need investors to keep the park's momentum going," Mr. Hatter said. "After you found Pierre, my friend, Duncan, here saw you talking to the news crew. He pulled me aside and agreed with me. It has to be you."

"It's true," Duncan said. "With your face, your innocent demeanor and your hesitation to accept any attention, you're the perfect candidate."

A tingling swept up the back of her neck. Heat bombarded her cheeks. How could he be that perceptive? "What do you mean the perfect candidate?"

Mr. Hatter reached for something on the desk behind him and held it toward her. Enlarged to at least fourteen by twenty in size, matted on black foam board, was what appeared to be an image from the original *Alice's Adventures in Wonderland*. It was a penciled sketch of a young girl staring straight forward, wearing a dress and pinafore, with tall grass and hollyhocks around her and carrying a pig in her arms.

The girl's face was innocent. Youthful and reticent, her forehead wide, her lips pouty giving her a sort of *who, me?* expression.

"I see it," Suzie said, perking up, glancing from the sketch to Adelie and back again. Her mouth widened in amazement. "It's so you. You could totally pull that off."

Adelie was at a total loss for words. Mr. Hatter propped the image up alongside the lamp on his desk and continued.

"When I first launched Wonderland, I hired an artist to recreate my mother's impressions of a book she loved for the signs for every ride, the entrance, even the directions throughout the parking lot. He did a great job for what it was, but the park has become campy. Everything is too exaggerated, too over-emphasized. Too cartoonish.

"I want it to become more *real* to those who arrive, and the way to do that is to redecorate. Rebrand. Ramp up the rides, the entire Wonderland experience."

"We believe a live actor would be the best way to handle that," Duncan said, stepping forward as if ready to enter the conversation. "Especially someone with your youthful, innocent demeanor. You capture the innocence of Alice, the curiosity mentioned multiple times throughout the book."

"'Curiouser and curiouser,'" Suzie mumbled.

Adelie's pulse clamored in her ears and a sudden coldness struck her to the center. Having an actual actor for the images was all well and good, but her? "I—I can't do that," she said in shock.

Mr. Hatter gave her a disarming smile. "I know it's coming out of nowhere for you. But we've been thinking about this for quite some time. If you really aren't interested at all, I'll send you off with your winnings and wish you the best. But I'm willing to add to your fifty-thousand-dollar reward."

Adelie's throat was dry enough to crack. "Add to it?"

"Of course. Models are always paid for their image. It's clear the chance for fame isn't appealing enough to you," Mr. Hatter said with a laugh. "To have your picture seen all over town, on brochures, our website, and even commercials—"

"You're talking about taking pictures of me?" Adelie wasn't sure why she hadn't grasped that to begin with. Her mind was a step behind. He couldn't be serious. She was no model. She'd loathed picture day growing up and begrudgingly had one senior picture taken because it'd been obligatory.

"Yes. It would involve a photo shoot. And I'm afraid money is all I have to offer. What might entice you to say yes? How does two-hundred and fifty-thousand sound?"

If Adelie had been holding something she would have dropped it. "Are you—?" She couldn't manage to finish.

No way. No way had she ever thought she'd even sniff that

much money, let alone touch it. Let alone hold it and have it to use. Along with a rush of breathlessness, other ideas flurried through her mind.

She could do so much with it. She could pay off their mortgage outright. She could pay the rest of Suzie's medical bills.

But photographs? Billboards? Adelie had witnessed the sheer number of attendants in the park today. Having that many people stare at her face, not only here but across the valley? Not to mention wherever else he would decide to advertise.

"Yes," Suzie blurted. "She'll do it."

Adelie's mouth gaped. "What? No, she won't do it."

"Miss Carroll," Mr. Hatter said, clearing his throat. "I'm not sure you understand—"

She stood, refusing to be simpered at. "No. Look, I'm really flattered, but this just isn't me. You could find a thousand other girls who would be better suited for this. They'd have experience; they'd have a…a desire for this. I don't want it."

She'd never been one to take center stage. She'd been on the light crew, on the sidelines feeding actors their lines. She'd never played a front role, and she had no interest in doing so now. That unnerving interview with the news crew was all the attention she ever wanted.

Suzie's face was a mashup of panic, disbelief, and desperation. She stood and shuffled forward; hands outstretched before her as though trying to hit the finish line first. She elbowed her way between Adelie and Mr. Hatter and linked her arm with Adelie's.

Suzie flashed an apologetic smile at Mr. Hatter. "Can you give us just a second?"

"What are you doing?" Adelie said through her teeth.

Suzie shushed her and guided her to the far corner, beyond the bar with a microwave and sink, to where a tall plant stood guard. She shot a look behind her shoulder before pinning her fiercest sisterly scowl on Adelie.

"Are you crazy?" she mumbled under her breath. "Just say yes."

Adelie worked to keep her voice low yet loud enough for only her sister to hear. "You can't accept for me. It's my face, not yours, that's going all over the place."

"Come on, why not? You are perfect. You found the rabbit. You've already been on the news. It would be even bigger for Wonderland, and that reward? Holy cow, Adelie, that would save Grandma and Grandpa's house. We wouldn't get foreclosed on."

Adelie couldn't deny the same thoughts had crossed her mind, but she'd stamped them out quick, like a dropped match in a forest. They could find some other way to save their home. She'd find a legitimate job, something that wouldn't require her to be so...out there.

"It's just a few pictures," Suzie went on, her tone turning corrective. "You heard what he said, you'll be all made up and Alice-y. No one will even recognize you otherwise." She threw out her hands and added a cheesy, encouraging smile.

Adelie scorned the temptation spurring inside of her. She loved her quiet life. But that was just it, if they lost their grandparents' house, it wouldn't be the life she loved. Quiet, solitude, in a place she'd lived her whole life, a place she longed to return to any time she left it.

This was her way to save it. With the money Mr. Hatter was offering, she and Suzie could buy it outright. They'd never get evicted again, and all that history, the memories of childhood, canning beans and picking raspberries, would be a daily walkthrough instead of a distant thought.

Just a few pictures. A few billboards—which were always up so high; who really looked at those anyway? It wasn't like this was anything salacious. She wasn't posing for Victoria's Secret, selling her soul or her body. Just her face.

Ugh. She couldn't do this. But how could she turn down a quarter of a million dollars?

Suzie's eyes were as wide as saucers. Her lower lip pouted. She'd mastered the pleading look, that was for sure.

"It's too bad they're not asking you." Adelie knuckled her sister's shoulder. Why couldn't they? Then again, Suzie was four years older. Not only that, Adelie couldn't ignore the compliments Mr. Hatter had paid her. *Her,* not Suzie. The withdrawn innocence, the sweetness yet standoffishness from that image. Suzie was so bubbly she'd just grin the entire time.

They needed someone pensive, someone absorbed and withdrawn. An unwanted confirmation nudged her at the thought. Much as she wanted to ignore it, something deep inside told her she could do it.

"But they're not asking me," Suzie said. "They want you. You can do this, Addy."

She closed her eyes. One slide at a time, she pictured their house being repainted, refurbished, fixed up and made their own. The decades-old plumbing that needed repairs, the cool air leaking through the antique windows. Both needed to be replaced, and neither of which could they even dream of affording, not while they were both in school. This way, they could be repaired, without Adelie or Suzie having to quit school or go into any more debt.

What if it turned out she was terrible at modeling? What if she ended up being exactly the opposite of what they thought they wanted?

The idea wedged in her chest like a fist. It pressed against her lungs, robbing their ability to draw in a full breath.

Two hundred and fifty thousand dollars, she told herself. *Just focus on that.*

"Okay," Adelie said, releasing the breath. "I'll do it."

Suzie fisted her hands and strangled a squeal halfway out of her throat, getting a grip on herself as Adelie gave her a pointed get-it-together glare. Adelie lifted her chin and strolled back to where Mr. Hatter and Mr. Hawthorne stood.

Adelie's palms were sweating like she was in the middle of summer. "Thanks for the offer, Mr. Hatter. If it's still on the table, I'd love to take you up on it."

There it was again. That zap-her-kneecap smile. This time it added an admiring glint in his green eyes that did strange things to her lower belly.

"Awesome," Mr. Hatter said. "I have some papers here for you to sign." He pulled them from atop his desk as well.

Adelie stiffened. Her head lightened; her thoughts went fuzzy. She forced herself not to glance at Suzie. "Right now?"

"Contracts, right?" Suzie asked, unfazed.

Trembling overtook Adelie as her brain slowly began to unplug. Why had she agreed? She was entirely not okay with this. It was too fast. She didn't have time to think things through, and she wasn't sure she wanted it anyway, not really.

A signature on a contract was final. Adelie's knees buckled. Suzie hurried to guide her to the nearest seat. She lowered her head and focused on breathing.

Mr. Hatter and Mr. Hawthorne exchanged a look before Mr. Hatter knelt before her. He rested a hand on her knee. The touch was a little forward, but nothing about him seemed to be conventional.

"I know this is a lot," he said, his tone gentle. "Why don't you take some time to think it through?"

Adelie didn't realize how much she was quivering until she pushed his hand from her knee. "How much time?"

Mr. Hatter sank onto his heels. "Two days?"

She laughed until she realized he was serious. She wiped her clammy palms on her thighs.

"I'd like to keep the momentum triggered by today's scavenger hunt going," he said. "If you don't want to be a part of that, I understand, but this could be the opportunity of a lifetime."

For me or for you? she wondered. Still, she couldn't deny the lure of the phrase he'd used. *Be a part of that.* Of this. Of Wonderland. She could be a part of something incredible, a living fairy tale, a live-action novel. She would *be* Alice.

The appearance of this entire offer turned on its head. Despite her anxieties, the glass was gradually becoming half full rather than half empty.

"Tell you what," Mr. Hatter said, standing to his full height and straightening his shirt. "Why don't you meet me here in Wonderland on Sunday? You can take this contract home and look it over. Will that give you enough time to think this over? The park will be closed. I'll give you a personal tour. Show you the areas I'll be updating and exactly where your images will go. Then, at that time, you can give me your decision. Does that sound reasonable?"

Suzie chewed her lip and practically leaped in place.

"That I can do," Adelie said. Some of the pressure the sight of the contract gave her released, and she took it from him.

Two days. She'd be touring Wonderland with its mouthwatering owner, and then she'd have to decide if she was ready to be in the public eye.

7

Adelie drummed her fingers on the dining table and stared. All those words. Usually, she loved reading, but that was fiction. Escape. This was more like a thesis paper on the benefits of filing a tax return. She had zero desire to read it, and once she signed, once she dotted every I and crossed every T, there would be no going back.

Seated on the chair beside her, Suzie passed her a mug of warm cider and gave her shoulder an encouraging squeeze. "It's okay," she said with the same tone she always used when something seemed too big to tackle. "You don't have to do this."

"Really?" It was exactly what Adelie wanted. An opening to back out.

"Sure," Suzie went on, relaxing in her chair and throwing an arm across the back. "It's only a quarter of a million dollars you're skipping out on. He'll just find some other girl who's more willing."

Adelie tugged on the sleeves of her sweater. She didn't like the words *some other girl.*

"You'll see someone else's face on the news or in the theme

park every time you pass it. And every time you pass it, you'll think: Hmm. That could have been me. Right, Fletch?"

Suzie rotated as her boyfriend, Fletcher, entered the kitchen with a newspaper tucked under his arm. His orange hair curled like a sponge. He was tall and gangly in a completely adorable way that made Suzie squirm.

"Huh?" Fletcher said, clueless.

Adelie rolled her eyes. "I get it. We need the money."

"Yes, we do." Suzie patted the contract like she would an obedient dog. Fletcher settled himself into the open seat beside her, and she slid him the remaining mug of cider.

"Thanks, babe," he said, crinkling open his newspaper and taking a sip. Adelie chuckled. Anyone who didn't know any better would think he lived here with them, he was over so often.

Suzie went on. "Not only that, but you know what I think? I think *you* need this."

"Yeah, like I need a bullet to the head."

Suzie leaned in, resting her elbows on the table, a feat which would have gotten her dismissed if it'd happened during dinner while they'd been growing up. "I'm serious. This is completely out of your comfort zone, but you're doing it, Addy. That takes gusto."

"Gusto?"

"Exactly. You know what Grandma always said. 'It's character-building to do one thing you don't like every day.' Look at all the character you'll be building."

"You're right," Adelie said with pluck, cottoning on to her sister's enthusiastic sarcasm. Oddly enough, her little pep talk was working. Her shoulders relaxed. She stopped fiddling with the end of her sleeves. "This is going to be good for me."

"What is?" Fletcher pried himself from his paper long enough to ask.

Suzie waved him off, keeping her attention on Adelie and promising to explain later.

How could this be good for her, though? Part of her still felt the way she had when she'd gone with some friends to a spook alley in high school. The pressure had been high. Everyone had laughed, prodding her, poking fun, taunting her to go. She'd been downright terrified, but she'd given in to the peer pressure. She'd gone through every frightening, too-dark inch of that freak show. When she'd arrived on the other side, she could have kissed every speck of light around.

Her friends had been wrong. Adelie hadn't gotten tougher. In fact, she'd sworn off creepy anything and had stuck to it.

Something told her this situation was going to be similar. Granted, she couldn't pass this chance up and risk finding someone else's face in Wonderland as a reminder of her lack of courage.

She had to do this. But that didn't mean anything about her was going to change.

～

Adelie stood at Wonderland's gates Sunday morning. The wrought iron curled in a quirky, mysterious way, implying darkness and mystery and yet playfulness within. Circles in the center of either side of the gate swirled with fancy Ws that connected to leaves and adjoining top hats.

A man in a plain uniform held a broom in one hand and a long-handled dustpan in the other. He shuffled his way over the pave stones that made up the front of the park, sweeping litter and other garbage that had drifted into Wonderland.

Rides that had taxied and spun within were now sleeping. The park wasn't open on Sundays, which was perfect for her.

She wouldn't have to deal with Mr. Hatter pressuring her to ride anything. Just a tour, that was all this was.

She would see the park. Get a better grasp of his intentions for its remodel. And then she would make her decision.

Adelie clutched her messenger bag—and the contract within it—and began to pace. He'd just said Sunday. No specific time. She probably should have clarified before leaving, but she had felt too self-conscious to contact him. She'd stewed over it the entire time during church, and now that she was here, she wondered if she should have called him sooner than a quick message of, *Hey, I'm heading over in a few minutes.*

How did she even know he got it? He hadn't responded.

Adelie could see several others working their way through the park's innards, stopping to wipe windows on the buildings, or to adjust the straps on tarps covering kiosks or change out garbage bags. She was starting to think she shouldn't have come at all when a smaller, regular-sized gate swung open twenty feet down the brick wall to her right.

Mr. Hatter stepped through, wearing jeans and a button-up shirt beneath a black leather jacket. His hair was tousled, his lips quirked, and with his left hand skimming his jeans pocket, he looked like the one who should be posing for pictures.

"Hey, there," he said. "I wasn't sure you were going to come."

She stepped toward him, her boots crunching on the sidewalk. "Hi, Mr. Hatter. Did you get my text?"

"Just a few minutes ago," he said. "Sorry about that. And please, call me Maddox."

She managed an agreeable nod.

"So, Adelie, are you ready?" he asked.

"R-ready?" She hated that she stammered whenever she was nervous or caught off-guard. It had always been an oddity of hers. Something she'd battled from the time she was young, even when she and Suzie had still lived with their parents.

"Yeah, the tour. Want to start at the beginning? Make our way through the park? I'll give you the inside scoop."

"That sounds good," she said. "Why don't you show me where the changes are going to be? You know, where you're going to put me. My pictures. I mean, where you're putting me. The pictures of me." Ugh. Could she get any more awkward?

Mr. Hatter's smile stretched only by a fraction, but enough to be noticeable.

"The beginning sounds great," she amended.

"*The Rabbit Hole* it is." Hands in his pockets, he invited her in and locked the door behind her.

It was hard to believe the park had been as crowded as it was the day of the scavenger hunt. Silence enveloped everything eerily now, in that way things that should have life and motion, but didn't. Adelie longed to break that silence. She asked the first question that came to her mind.

"Your name. Is it really your name? Hatter is legitimate?"

"It is," he said. "My mom named me Maddox because *Alice's Adventures in Wonderland* was her favorite book. In fact, this—" He gestured. "Is all for her."

Adelie stopped for a moment to admire the flowerbeds, trees, and towering rides. The smells of popcorn and caramel were missing today. She was surprised she'd noticed, considering how distracted she'd been the last time she was here. She hadn't taken much time to really *see* everything Friday, either.

"Really? That's such an amazing thing to do for your mom. Does she love to come here?"

Maddox lowered his head. "She passed away, I'm afraid. It's one reason I did it, as a tribute to her memory."

"I'm sorry to hear it. That's so hard. Both of my parents are gone too," Adelie said, falling into step with him once more. Why had she brought that up? She didn't want to go into her family's difficult past—not now, not ever. And especially not with him. In fact, part of her wanted to forget she'd had parents at all.

Maddox led the way up the stairs toward the entry point for *The Rabbit Hole* drop. No lines. Just directly to the front. She remembered some of her frustration with the lines, regretting how surly and distracted she'd been. Part of her wished for a do-over. How would it be to jump on any ride you want whenever you wanted?

"I'm sorry to hear that," he said.

"Yeah, I was raised by my grandparents. That's one reason I'm doing this. I want to save their house."

He whistled. "Must be some house."

"It is," she said, unable to help her smile. "It's got this perfect craftsman look to it, and I have so many memories there."

"I'd like to see it sometime," he said.

Adelie paused. "You would?"

"Sure. If you care about it that much, then it must be amazing. All right, here we go." He gestured to the sign at the front of the ride near the railing meant to separate those who were waiting from those taking their turns.

It was a lighthearted version of Alice on her hands and knees, staring into a hole in the side of a bank. "This is the sign we'll be redoing. I want to hail back to as many of the original images from the book as possible. We'd like to capture you looking stunned and amazed as you're falling slowly down a well."

The idea made her muscles twitch.

"I see," she said. "How exactly are you going to capture me falling?"

Maddox lifted his arms and mimed the movement, astonished facial expression and all. The combined actions were so endearing, she laughed.

"You're onto something. Why not just don a wig and do the pictures yourself?" she said.

"And miss the chance of seeing you?" He winked, kinking her insides. "Come on. *Pool of Tears* is next."

They meandered through, stopping by the water ride she and Suzie had experienced. She was grateful the towering, quick-drop ride was closed. She'd ridden it Friday to obtain the next clue, and once was enough. They stopped next at the *Caucus Race* ride, made up of animals that spun and moved at slow speeds.

"To dry off," Maddox added as he pointed them out.

Adelie chuckled to herself, remembering the ride's slow-spin progression and the young kids and their parents who'd smiled in delight. It was the perfect sort of ride for little kids.

"It's nice of you to gear some rides to kids," she said.

"People from every walk of life love the book. And if not the book, then Disney's rendition of the story. I wanted to make sure the park could be a family place."

"Is that why you're not open on Sunday?"

"An old-fashioned notion, I guess," he said, stopping before the *Odds N' Ends* store across from the *Ever After Sweet Shoppe*. "Mind if I make a confession?"

She swallowed. "What do you mean?"

"I saw you in the shop Friday," he said, gesturing toward *Odds N' Ends* with its sweeping striped awning. "You stole my breath, right from the start."

Talk about stealing breath. Her lips parted. She was captivated by his confession, by the sincerity in his eyes. What did *that* mean? Who talked like this anyway, especially to someone he just met?

"I—I don't know what to say."

The corner of his mouth tipped. "I knew from that moment I needed you as my Alice."

She shook the stardust from her eyes. Right. Alice. He was only talking about his park.

Adelie drew in a long breath and stepped away from him, waiting for her head to clear. *Don't get in over your head,* she told herself, staring at the brick. She needed a focal point, to get herself back on track away from the cloud he'd momentarily led her on.

Maddox pointed to the store's windows.

"See? Even here, you'll be on posters and displays in the store windows. Even the bags in the stores will have some version of you on them."

Butterflies rolled in her stomach but were soon forgotten as thunder crackled through the sky overhead. March was the season for spring showers. Seconds later, a single drop kissed Adelie's cheek. She blinked upward, struck by the mass of gray clouds that closed in overhead. They hadn't been there when she'd first arrived.

"Uh-oh," Maddox said. "Looks like we might have to cut things short unless you want to get caught in a deluge."

"Spring rain," Adelie said with a chuckle. More drops trickled down, wetting her hair and shoulders. Without further warning, the rain increased its tempo, drumming down against the rooftops and tinkling against what sounded like tin. She lifted her messenger bag above her head as puddles at their feet quickly formed.

"Here," Maddox called in the din. He put a hand on the small of her back, and the two ran toward the carousel about twenty feet away.

Adelie followed Maddox, who wove his way through the iron maze for patrons to line up within. He opened the final gate, allowing her through first to hurry up the step and onto the dormant carousel, taking shelter beneath its circus-tent-like roof.

The air was still brisk, and the rain made a symphony of noise on the roof, but at least she wasn't getting any more soaked than she already was. Adelie lowered her bag, wiped wet hair and rain from her eyes, and caught her racing breath.

Rain dripped from Maddox's hair, which had fallen into his eyes. He raked his hands through, whipping it clear of his forehead. In his leather jacket, with his watch peeking through the end of his sleeve, the action made him appear like a supermodel. Tantalizing, but off-limits.

"Here we go," he said, resting a hand on the back of a seahorse. "We'll just wait it out."

"This is actually really great," Adelie said, reining in her racing heart and glancing at the carousel.

"It is?"

She gestured to the surrounding animals; the mice, cats, flamingoes, and then up at the inner workings of the poles leading to their gears in the roof. This ride hadn't been part of Friday's challenge, which was a shame. She would have loved a ride.

"How often does anyone get a carousel all to themselves?"

"You've got your pick," Maddox said, gesturing to the animals.

The prospect was enchanting. Despite the cold, warmth radiated through her at his invitation.

"No horses?" she asked. "All carousels have horses."

"Not this one." He gripped the pole holding a fat hedgehog to the upper and lower gears.

"Makes sense," she said, wandering on the wide, circular platform and inspecting each ornate creature. "Wonderland doesn't conform to any norms."

"Exactly," Maddox said, walking with her as she wove between a pair of elaborate fish. "Which one will it be?"

"This one," Adelie said, stopped beside a brilliantly colored peacock. Peacocks were the kind of bird that demanded respect and attention, yet they kept to themselves. She liked that.

"Well?" He inclined his head. "Are you going to get on?"

A blush claimed her cheeks. She lowered her head, hoping to hide it. "It's not moving."

The corner of his lip quirked. "Isn't it?"

Adelie fought a smile and lifted a foot, climbing onto the peacock. She gripped the pole with one hand to steady herself until she inserted her feet into the stirrups on either side. Seated as she was, it put her on eye-level with Maddox.

Rain hammered against the carousel roof and created a curtain around them. For only a moment, Adelie didn't notice the playful landscapes painted on the carousel's center pivot. Her feet nestled in the stirrups, her hand gripped the peacock's reins, and her heart tapped out a rapid rhythm in her chest.

Maddox hadn't found his own creature as she thought he would. He remained close and directed his gaze at her. Lifting a hand, he gently wiped a raindrop from her cheek. His touch sizzled straight into her skin.

He sees me as his Alice, she reminded herself. *Nothing more.*

"Would you believe I've never been on a carousel before?" she asked.

His hand rested on the peacock's fiberglass beak. "How is that even possible?"

She tried to play it off as something totally normal. "I've never really been anywhere like this. To a theme park, I mean."

"Where are you from?" he asked.

"Here," she said. "Westville. I've lived here my whole life. I just—" How could she tell him she didn't get out much, and that it was by choice? She might as well proclaim she opted to live the most boring life possible because it meant less risk.

"If I knew how it worked, I'd start it for you," he said, still standing close to her.

Adelie swallowed. She'd never had attention like this before, not from boys at school or men in her college classes—the ones that were in person or online, like she was taking right now. She'd never even been kissed, either. The prospect had been non-existent. But here, in the rain, on a carousel that for all the world was singing its own melody and spinning right off with her imagination, a kiss suddenly became an option.

He was *so* handsome. And he was looking at her, resting his hand close to hers, her knee brushing his side.

The rain slowed. Her mind cleared in the subsequent quiet. What was she doing thinking of kissing him?

"Looks like things are clearing up out there," he said.

"Yeah. I should probably get going."

But she didn't move, and for a long moment, neither did he. He lingered there, capturing her with his pale green eyes.

Finally, he cleared his throat and stepped back, glancing around as if only just remembering where he was. "Right," he said, offering her a hand as she slid down.

She didn't take it. She wasn't sure she could handle feeling his fingers touch hers.

Clearing his throat, Maddox stuffed his hands into his pockets. "I think you get the idea of what we'll be doing here. Was two days enough time? Have you made a decision about my offer?"

Adelie tucked her wet hair behind her ear. "When would I get the money?"

"Half up front," Maddox said. "And half will be deposited once the images are in place, in the bank account of your choice."

Half. Oh, sweet goodness.

She attempted to remain unperturbed, though inside her organs were rotating. "When would the photo shoot be?"

"One week," Maddox said. He stepped off from the carousel's

platform and again turned to offer her a hand, but she'd already leaped off as well. "And then you'll be in every corner of Wonderland."

Every corner. She was really doing this. "Will I need any kind of... I don't know, training?"

Maddox stood back. He rested a hand in his chin and narrowed his eyes, shrewdly examining her.

Adelie gripped the soaked strap of her messenger bag. "What are you doing?"

His eyes narrowed. He still hadn't taken them from her. "If you're asking me whether you can stand there, looking bewildered, lost, and beautiful all at once, I think you've got it mastered."

Adelie's lips parted. She didn't know what to say.

"The whole premise of *Alice in Wonderland* is this fantastic dream for Alice," Maddox said. "Let me make this a dream for you."

Whew. A dream, sure. A dream Alice had wanted to wake from the entire time. A dream where everyone she encountered was borderline psychotic. Still, Adelie felt as though she'd drunk from that bottle. She was soaring, feet higher than her normal height so her head wafted in the clouds.

She must be crazy to agree to this, but her lips formed the words all on their own.

"Yes. Okay. I'll do it."

Maddox's smile was a flash of lightning across a bleary sky. Vibrant, colorful, and so intense it stole every ounce of her attention and made her heart hiccup. Now that was a smile.

Lifting the flap on her messenger bag, she removed the contract and signed it there on the puddled Wonderland street. Maddox accepted it when she was finished, tucking into his jacket to retrieve what looked like a business card.

"Come to this location next Monday," he said, offering her the card with an address on it.

Somehow, her fingers closed around it. "What should I wear?"

"Everything will be set up for you," he said, walking her to the exit. Their return trip was quiet, filled with anticipation and uncertainty. They passed the rides and kiosks she'd noticed before, and the men who'd been cleaning the streets had vanished, probably taking shelter during the brief storm.

The park's elegant entrance came into view, and soon Maddox opened the side door for her with a set of keys from his pocket.

"Okay," she breathed, nervous.

"Okay," he replied, the corner of his lips quirking and adding an extra glint in his eyes.

Dipping her chin, Adelie thanked him for the tour and bade him goodbye.

She ambled in a daze to her car's space in the mostly empty parking lot. So much had happened and in so short a time. She couldn't believe the afternoon they'd shared. The rain, the carousel, the contract. She'd signed it and handed it to Maddox. That meant this was official. That meant in one more week, it would be time to become Alice.

8

Adelie approached the security booth, which was located at the end of the street address Maddox had given her—and rolled her car window down. A man in a blue suit with patches on the shoulders and a stern forehead scowled at her. A silver nametag secured over his breast pocket read, *Juan Ramirez*.

"Miss Carroll?"

"Y-yes. That's me."

He examined something on his screen, possibly comparing her face to a picture, though where he would have gotten one, she couldn't say. Then again, she had been on the news after her completely unexpected victory.

"They're expecting you," he said with a nod. Giving her what she assumed was a smile, he added, "Welcome to Mr. Hatter's estate."

Adelie inclined her head and the gate swung open. She wished it would open quicker. The guard was so stern, he might as well be made from steel. Then again, if she had security of any kind, she'd want its director to be no-nonsense and threatening at first glance too.

She passed through and rolled down the remainder of the long drive. The extensive grounds were green and lush and spread for what seemed like miles along the distance between the guard's station and the massively huge mansion.

It was like a miniature castle, set off by pointed dormers above an arched courtyard that led to what must be the front door. Balconies, turrets along the rooftop, and multiple stone stairways connected by a path that passed dozens of windows in every size speckling the exterior added variety to the bronze stones.

Adelie took a moment—or a thousand—to stop and just stare. She wanted to soak in every detail and appreciate each stunning aspect, from the windows to the intricate shapes in the stones, for what each individual aspect added to the whole. She couldn't imagine living in a place like this. Visiting it was one thing, but having it for a home? It was breathtaking.

A few other cars were already parked in the drive. Adelie pulled between the smaller black Lexus and the large white, windowless van. She cut the ignition and stared at her hands' ten- and two o'clock position on the steering wheel. She needed to go inside. To let go of the wheel, exit the vehicle and *move*.

Her phone buzzed from its place on the dashboard, startling her. Suzie's name filled the screen, along with a dozen emojis trumpeting her cause and cheering her on. Bolstered by the well-timed text, Adelie smiled. Suzie had to work, but at least she was there in emoji, if not in spirit.

"Just one step at a time," Adelie told herself. Exhaling through a small part in her lips, she pulled the car door's handle and stepped out into the chilly spring morning.

A decadent fountain across from the courtyard stood like its own version of the Eiffel Tower—a sight Adelie had always longed to see in real life. Water spewed from multiple tiers and made an umbrella around a collection of stones.

Her old Honda looked like a crushed soda can compared to the Lexus, whose chrome handles and bumper were not only *not* dented but shined to beat the stars. That wasn't a good sign. She hadn't even bothered doing herself up, since Maddox had said she would be getting a makeover, but now, here, she felt like a shabby, discarded rag beside an exquisite gown.

What was she doing here? She didn't belong in a place like this.

"You can do this," she told herself. Grandma Carroll's house. She was doing this to save her home.

It took much more effort than it should have to approach the enormous, mahogany door. More so to lift a hand and ring the doorbell, but she managed it. A grand sound pealed like a gong, as if meant to reach the expansive ends of such a huge dwelling.

"Though he probably has a butler or something," she muttered to herself, fighting away the thought of Maddox Hatter leaping and sprinting from the far end of his house just to answer the door. The thought made her smile.

The door opened to reveal an older man with salt and pepper hair in a fine-fitted suit and a conservative brown tie. An earpiece coiled from his left ear and beneath his collar. Not exclusively a butler then, but more security.

"Miss Carroll? I'm Randy Kirk, but you can call me Kirk."

"H-hi, Kirk."

Unlike Juan's stern, no-nonsense greeting, he smiled. The sight chiseled away at the hard nervousness inside her. "Please come in. Mr. Hatter and Mr. Hawthorne are waiting with the hairdresser, though I believe a wig-maker is on hand as well, if you prefer."

Her mouth gaped. "A-a wig *maker*?"

She was having a hard time following his thought process *and* taking in the vaulted foyer at the same time. The white and cream interior was set off by dark wood along the ceiling's edge, the window frames, and the doors. Swirled, wrought iron curled around the staircase and led to a magnificent window on the landing above. Adelie itched to explore, to venture through and investigate every nook and cranny in this incredible place.

Kirk gave her a knowing smile. "They're just down here, if you'd like to follow me."

Adelie forced her feet forward. This place was too perfect to be real, and so opposite from the blend of beauty and chaos in Maddox's Wonderland she couldn't keep her jaw from dropping.

The ceiling along the wide, bright corridor was curved, set off again by that dark wood. Fantastic chandeliers dangled and teased their light upon her, and she kept looking, looking, looking everywhere she possibly could. An elegant set up of tables and chairs here. A fireplace there. Vases of flowers, columns, and paintings, so much splendor in one place.

Kirk took a series of short stairs and turned down another hall leading to a widespread room. Windows splashed sunlight on every surface and left shadows nowhere to hide.

A pair of double doors led out onto what she assumed was a balcony. They were situated across from the stone fireplace, which stretched to high-five the vaulted ceiling above. Maddox, Duncan, and a woman Adelie hadn't yet met chuckled in low tones beside the fireplace, and the sound fisted her stomach.

The woman's hair was stylish, her clothes well-fitted and hip. Her jeans were cropped short, and she wore a shirt with tassels dangling along the hem.

Mid-laugh, Maddox turned, his face brightening at the sight of her.

"Adelie," he said with delight.

Embarrassment bloomed in her cheeks, and a small firework exploded in her stomach. She hadn't been able to stop thinking about the simmering effect he'd had on her during their tour, and especially the romantic moment they'd shared on the carousel. It had all seemed so surreal but seeing him here now cemented everything in like concrete.

She was at his house. And he was looking at her as though she'd been the reason for the sunrise that morning.

"Hey," she said.

The woman closed in, arms folded, heels clacking on the floor. She analyzed Adelie from head to toe.

"You're right," she said, her expression growing more and more in approval by the minute. "She is going to be perfect."

Maddox's, Duncan's, and the woman's gazes each fixed on her. Her breathing accelerated and she fought the urge to chew on her fingernails. Oh boy. What was Adelie getting herself into? If she couldn't handle the attention from Maddox and his wig maker—or whoever this woman was—how could she ever handle having so much attention on her everywhere else?

Her throat closed over every word as she attempted to push it out. "Sorry, I didn't get ready or anything. I wasn't sure exactly what I was supposed to wear."

"You look amazing," Maddox said. "Just how you're supposed to. This is Cathy. She's a genius when it comes to hair and makeup. The photographer will be here in two hours. Does that give you ladies enough time to do what you need to?"

Two hours? Photographer? That wasn't enough time. She wasn't ready.

"Should be enough," Cathy said, sizing Adelie up with one hand gripping her chin.

Adelie wished she could get a handle on her thoughts. And her breathing, for that matter.

"I—"

"Do you need anything?" Maddox said.

Her vision blanked. The room shrunk, bringing a wave of irrational dizziness with it. She was thirsty, so thirsty. She needed some air, or perhaps a drink of water. That would help her quivering insides.

"C-can I talk to you for a second?"

Maddox's face softened and he guided her to the opposite corner of the room. She ignored Cathy and Mr. Hawthorne's puzzled exchange and tried not to trip over her own feet the way she had during a presentation in her English class last semester.

Her internal temperature had flared up, just like this. Her body had tingled, her mind turning white, just like this. She'd stumbled on her way out of the classroom, feeling more embarrassed than ever. It was one thing for her anxiety to flare up as a child, but as a grown woman? What was her problem?

"Is everything okay?" Maddox asked, tucking his hands into his pockets, as cool as a cucumber.

She really wished she could sit down for a minute. "I don't know," she said. "I thought I could do this, but now? Seeing where you live? Being in the moment? I just—"

As if reading her earlier thoughts, he reached for a bottle of water on a nearby end table and handed it to her.

"It's normal to be nervous," he said. "And you did sign the contract."

She bobbed her head and took the water, broke it open, then took a grateful sip. The cool liquid helped calm her somewhat inside. "I know. I know I did."

He put his warm hands on her shoulders. "Adelie. Look at me."

Blood palpitating, she lifted her head as though it was connected to a weight on the floor. His direct gaze had a mesmerizing effect, but it wasn't enough to soothe her nervousness about this. She willed herself to feel as comfortable around him now as she'd been on the carousel in the rain. That had been so relaxed. So private.

This was the complete opposite. If only Suzie had been able to come.

Against her will, childhood memories flashed; memories with her father, who'd been far less kind than Maddox was at this moment. She pushed the memories aside.

"I wish I could tell you that you don't have to do this. I suppose I could find a way to nullify our contract if that's what you really want. But I need you to ask yourself what you really want."

She didn't have to ask herself. She wanted to go home, to cuddle up and forget the world and everyone in it for a while with a good book. Or perhaps to go over the syllabus for her new medical terminology course.

But how much longer would she even have a home? As if reading her thoughts, Maddox said, "Remember your grandparents' house? I can't help you save it unless you help me."

She was touched he remembered, and at his soothing tone, she relaxed.

"Right," she said on an exhale.

"You'll be fine," he said. "More than that, you'll be amazing."

In spite of the confidence in his words, her uneasiness grew. "I—whew. Sure."

His mouth pressed into a line. He shifted his weight. "Want to tell me what's bothering you about all of this?"

This was mortifying. How could she lay out her insecurities for him? She'd buried them as well as she could for years now, but the more time she spent with Maddox, the more her locked time capsule was becoming more like perforated Styrofoam. Living solo with her sister didn't help. Maddox was forcing her out of her shell, and she felt more vulnerable than she had in years.

Never mind her difficult childhood. She wouldn't go into that with him. She decided to stick with a different truth.

"I've never been the leading act," she said. "I'm the supporting role."

"I see." He darted a glance in Duncan and Cathy's direction before shifting as if to shield her from them and mumbled, "What if you're more than you think you're meant to be?"

He sounded so sincere. So genuine it scared her. Her eyes widened. He couldn't know what he was saying. He barely knew *her*. "What does that mean?"

A shrug. "I mean, sometimes we have to take risks to make amazing things happen."

He was unbelievable. The conversation was diverting enough she forgot her anxiety for the moment. "And you? What are you risking?"

Without hesitation, he declared, "Nothing."

That was a football field away from the truth. She thought of this exorbitant home of his. His outlandish but incredible theme park. He had *so much* to lose. What did he mean he wasn't risking anything here?

"I—I'm sorry. I'm not sure I understand."

Hands in his pockets, he never took his attention from her. "Because of you, I know I'm not risking a thing. I'm one-hundred percent sure about you."

She wasn't sure if it was because of the intensity of his gaze, the effect of their surroundings, or the promise that losing money on her account wasn't even a risk. Whatever it was, she was struck by his statement. He was that confident in her?

Her?

Adelie Eleanor Carroll, the small-town wonder who'd never won anything in her life, who'd never been kissed, who'd never stepped out of her comfort zone because fear's shadow was always bigger than any prospect of victory. She'd always taken the back row at church, and she'd never had enough confidence in herself to try for anything she might fail at.

Her lack of confidence had been why she'd lost her job in retail. Why she'd botched every interview afterward.

Maddox didn't care about all that. He didn't *know* about all that. At this moment, he cared about *her*. He wanted her, and his confidence was more bolstering than anything she'd ever experienced.

Her body relaxed. Lightness blossomed in her chest. He thought she could do it. And suddenly, she wanted to.

"Okay," she said with surprising assurance.

What if this was an opportunity in ways other than monetarily? She could become a different version of herself. Test the waters. See what it took and what she might gain, instead of focusing on everything she might lose.

"You're sure?" he clarified.

Her blood slowed. Clarity settled into her mind. "Yes. I'm sure."

Maddox's eyes turned a shade of approval. The warm, reassuring glance sent a trickle of hope and something like intrigue along her spine and into her stomach. His hand found hers. His skin soft, he squeezed just enough. The soothing touch brought a sting of tears to her eyes.

No man had ever shown interest in her before. But just like back at the carousel, she wouldn't mistake this for something more than it was. This was business. She was nothing more than the face he wanted for his park, and she had to always remember that.

"Thanks," she said.

Keeping her hand in his, he guided her back to where Duncan and Cathy waited.

"She's all yours," Maddox told Cathy.

The bracelets along Cathy's wrist jangled as she gestured to the leather couch. "Want to sit down?"

Adelie took the offered seat. Cathy sat across from her and gathered Adelie's hands in hers.

"Our boy Maddox wants you to keep much of what you've already got going, but he did ask me to prepare you for the photo shoot. Mind if we sprinkle on some makeup and trim your hair just a bit? I might also add some highlights. Make sure it's extra blonde. Our girl Alice is blonde in the book."

"Highlights?" Her breath hitched.

Cathy quirked a brow. "Is that a problem?"

Adelie doubted it would matter if it was. She shook her head. "No, that's fine." She'd never had highlights before either.

Cathy offered a friendly, impish smile that managed to inject an additional dose of comfort to Adelie. Though she didn't know her, Adelie suspected the look implied confidence in her as well. In *her*. Adelie. "You'll hardly recognize yourself when I'm done. Come on."

9

Maddox checked his watch for what seemed like the hundredth time. He'd said two hours, but Cathy and Adelie had been at this for closer to three. How could it take this long?

He couldn't help but remember the fear in Adelie's demeanor when she'd first arrived. Maybe he'd made a mistake putting so much on her so quickly. She'd made it unmistakably clear she didn't want this. He should never have pushed her into it or encouraged her the way he had.

But the gleam in her eyes when he'd said those words... He'd lit a fire in her. He could see her desire to be someone different from who she was. It was almost like belief, like the compliments he paid her were the first she'd ever received. That drew her to him. In some bizarre, mystical way, he wanted to shower her with attention. Didn't she know how special she was?

He hadn't been acquainted with her long enough to know the extent of her deeper qualities himself, but after their afternoon in the park, getting caught in the rain with her and seeing her endearing excitement about the carousel, he hadn't been able to think of anyone else since.

Were her nerves the reason for her delay? Was she okay? Cathy would be careful, he knew. He'd nearly stormed in to check on her several times, but Ritchie, the photographer, arrived, and Maddox got distracted.

Now Ritchie was ready. He'd transformed the ballroom into a studio, complete with backdrop and props.

Adelie's hesitation, her caution and timidity, made Maddox want to cradle her in his arms and assure her he would protect her and help her. He wasn't sure why—though he suspected it had something to do with his mother. She'd had trouble with crowds as well, and his father had always given her a hard time for it. His mom had told him how grateful she was to have Maddox there.

For Adelie, he knew putting herself out there for a photo shoot took more courage than she thought she had, but he saw something in her from the minute he'd spotted her in the gift shop. Then, he'd witnessed the same spark in her as she'd settled onto the squat stool beside the March Hare's table. People claimed they could read others' auras, and while he'd never given the claims much backing, he would now. He couldn't deny the sight of Adelie had *called* to him. Maddox was eager for Cathy to bring that spark out for everyone else as well.

Footsteps sounded from the hall outside. Maddox exhaled, doing his best to act casual and like he wasn't a tornado inside. Ritchie also stood and pocketed his phone, watching the door with expectation.

Cathy entered first, wearing a black, stylist's apron she hadn't had on earlier. A blue comb and pair of scissors jutted from the wide front pocket. Breath bated, Maddox stiffened as Adelie entered after.

Combed away from her face and secured by a headband, her yellow hair tumbled in gentle waves to her shoulders. Its color was lighter, set off with highlights, and added a glow to

Adelie's countenance. Or maybe that was the way Cathy had arranged her makeup. Either way, she had created a youthful masterpiece. In the blue dress with its poufy skirt, the white pinafore over the top, and the red stripes along the hem? It was as though the Alice he'd seen in pictures his entire life had grown up.

The gleam in her blue eyes. The bright flicker of delight, the bashful blush pinking up her cheeks when her gaze aligned with his. Heat flushed across Maddox's skin.

"Do you think this will work?" Adelie asked, tugging on the skirt.

Maddox had to clear his throat before he could speak. "You're perfect."

"Perfect?"

"You'll make the perfect Alice, I mean."

She dipped her chin.

"That," Ritchie said, interrupting the chemistry swirling between them. He pointed a finger in her direction, camera in his other hand, before directing her to the bright studio setup with its green screen background. "Come here, young lady, and do what you just did."

The instant Adelie set foot on the set, her head dropped. Her lips tucked into her teeth. Ritchie gave instruction after instruction, but no matter what he did, no matter how he posed her, she wouldn't loosen up. Maddox wanted to go to her, to put his arm around her and assure her she would be okay, to help her relax, but he didn't dare interfere.

"There," Ritchie said, offsetting his feet and holding the camera over his eye. "That's—no. No. Not like that. Go back to what you were just doing. Ugh."

Ritchie's tone grew exasperated.

"Sorry." She hugged her arms to her chest as if trying to fold herself in half. "I told him I wouldn't be very good at this."

"You're doing just fine," Maddox assured, hoping she believed him.

Ritchie lowered the camera. "This is not working. Why don't you take a break? We'll all take a break. Get some air." He set his camera down on its case near one of the tripod stands beside a light surrounded by a wide, circular shade, and strutted out of the room, his assistant scurrying after.

Color blotched Adelie's cheeks. She took advantage of Ritchie's absence and dashed from the set and back onto the tile with the desperation of a sailor eager to reach land.

Her blue eyes swam with worry. "I'm so sorry," she told Maddox.

He placed his hands on her arms. "You're doing just fine," he said in his calmest tone. "This is all new. Ritchie is just used to working with more experienced models."

She winced, and he cursed himself.

Why had he said that? Maddox hurried to correct himself. "I mean, this is your first time doing anything like this. No one expects you to get it right the first time."

She bobbed her head, her stare fixated on his collar. "I feel so silly. There aren't even any props or the backdrops he's talking about. Like the trees? How can I look at a tree when there isn't one? I'm just pantomiming, and I have no idea what I'm doing."

Maddox's jaw clenched for a moment. He hadn't thought she'd need training, but he should have clued her in a little more about what would be expected. That was clear now. He'd wanted to speed through the process and get things rolling as quickly as possible, but maybe he'd rushed into this. Maybe they should postpone the shoot, give Adelie some time to better prepare herself.

"Break's over," Ritchie called, reentering the room. His tone sounded infinitely more chipper than it had when he'd stormed out.

Adelie's eyes squeezed shut.

"You ready to try again?" Maddox asked.

Her expression pleaded with him, but words fled. Instead, she gave him a shrug and shuffled toward the studio.

Maddox wanted to swoop in, tell Ritchie he'd made a mistake, and rescue her. He couldn't embarrass her like that. She was trying her best. Ritchie was already here, all set up. They might as well start again.

Arms folded, hand on his chin, Ritchie called without turning. "Hatter? Get over here."

Confused, but willing to do what he could, Maddox strode to the photographer's side. "You need me?"

"Yeah." Though Ritchie addressed Maddox, his attention was on Adelie. Head bowed, she lifted her lashes in Maddox's direction. Soft pink climbed in her cheeks.

"There it is again," Ritchie said, softer this time. He faced Maddox. "Stay here by my side and keep her looking at you."

"At *me*?" Maddox said in surprise. "Why?"

Ritchie smiled through his goatee. "You bring out the blush in her."

Adelie must have heard him. Once again, her cheeks went bright pink. She shifted her posture.

"There! Like that, it's perfect. Don't move." Ritchie worked around her, snapping photo after photo. "Good, now reach upward to the tree."

"But there is no tree," she said, confused.

"Don't worry, there will be."

Maddox crossed his arms over his chest, hoping she was thinking of the same thing he was. Of the way he'd jokingly mimed lifting his arms and posing during their tour of the park. He winked at her, and she gave him that coy, reserved smile and turned as though reaching for an invisible apple.

Though there was no background, he pictured it exactly as

he'd done the first time he'd seen her sitting at the table outside the March Hare's house. The magic of the moment swirled through his mind, bringing an imaginary scene to life. She was stardust and enchantment, and he was captivated. There it was. There was the magic he knew was in her.

The camera made click after click sounds, and the more the shoot went on, the more relaxed Adelie seemed to become. It ended with her walking toward Ritchie, her attention focused at something invisible to her side while fans blew air to lift her hair away from her face.

Ritchie's camera made a final clicking noise before he lowered it. "That's it," he said with a pronounced exhale. "That was amazing." He turned to Maddox. "Boss?"

Clearly asking for approval, Maddox gave it. He'd been spellbound by her the entire time.

"Enchanting," Maddox agreed, shaking hands with Ritchie.

Ritchie signaled his crew, and the gathered men and women began packing up lights and the set in such an orderly fashion it was clear they'd done it a thousand times before. Adelie meandered to the window and glanced out, and Maddox dodged between a pair of men carrying black cases toward her.

"You did it," he said.

Adelie peered at him over her shoulder. "Yeah," she said.

He waited for her to elaborate, but she didn't continue.

He hurried to fill the awkward silence. Part of him ached to know what she thought of the shoot after it was all said and done. "If you'd like to go change, I can meet you out in the foyer when you're done," he offered.

Tension seeped from her. She faced him, directing the full force of her blue eyes on him, before she inclined her head and made her way out of the room.

~

Adelie changed into her regular clothes, but as she looked in the mirror, it wasn't only the makeup and highlights that made her feel like a new person. She was taller somehow. She'd done something difficult, something that scared her. It hadn't been like the spook alley, where she was more terrified when it was over than she'd been at the start. No, this time, she was soaring inside.

She'd never been one to bask under the weight of attention, but Maddox's was riveting. From the minute they'd met, his gaze spoke volumes. Every glance glimmered with interest and admiration. She'd tried playing it off as something else, but what else could it be? It was curiosity and adventure, as though he had plans to rove and explore new territory, and he wanted to bring her along.

Throughout the entire photo shoot, any time nerves had plucked her or attempted to sever her concentration, all she had to do was look at him. To see the glimmer of wonder and weakness in his gaze, it'd been enough to melt the most solid unease inside her.

She'd felt courageous, spontaneous, and stouthearted with him. Adelie had never been strong or resolute in her life, but he gave her the impression that maybe, just maybe, she could be.

She wasn't sure what to do now that the shoot was over. Maddox had said to meet him in the foyer, so she folded the dress, apron, and the tulle underskirt as nicely as she could, left them on the chair in the room she'd changed in, and headed that direction.

Settling on the foyer's lavish bench, she watched Ritchie and his crew haul case after case out to the white van. When his supplies were all packed in, Ritchie returned and took her hand. Adelie hurried to her feet once more. Not for the first time, she noticed his fingernails were painted black.

"It was lovely to meet you," the photographer said. "I can't wait for the finished product."

Adelie opened her mouth to reply when Maddox approached and clapped Ritchie on the shoulder. His presence sent a jolt through her. She had tunnel vision, barely able to take in anything but the billionaire.

What had Maddox thought of Ritchie's comments during the shoot? Time after time, Ritchie had pointed out her reaction to Maddox's attention. She hadn't been able to help it. His effect on her was increasing the more time she spent around him. What had Maddox thought of it?

"Nicely done," Maddox said as Ritchie drove away.

She linked her fingers in front of her and placed her palms against her stomach. "Thanks, that was kind of amazing."

"Better than you thought?"

Only because you were there. She tucked a hair behind her ear. "Yeah, actually. When will the images be done?"

He glanced out the large window where the fountain was visible. "I've got Ritchie on a tight schedule. It'll take some time to get everything printed and up, but I can show them to you when everything is ready."

"That would be great," she said. "Just, you know, give me a call." Give her a call. She'd invited Maddox to call her.

For a moment she wished their situation was different. That he was interested in her because of who she was, not because of who he wanted her to be. He would have asked for her number. She would have given it, and maybe that staggering chemistry they'd shared on the carousel would be real.

She stood before him in anticipation, wondering how to go about bidding him goodbye. Things seemed to be different between them after the shoot. Should she hug him? Offer to shake his hand?

Adelie knew she shouldn't care this much. He was only interested in her for his park, but their attraction was undeniable. Did he feel it too?

"I'll walk you out," he said, one hand in his pocket, the other indicating his fancy front door.

Adelie bit her lip. It would be better to leave things this way, without any walking to cars or awkward goodbyes. Their relationship needed to end here. She would wait for word on the pictures, and that would be that.

"I'm okay," she told him. "Thanks again."

He stuffed his other hand into his pocket. His expression betrayed a hint of desire, that he wanted to say something else, to declare the emotion collecting in his eyes, but Adelie pressed her lips together, gave him a final nod, and strolled toward the door.

She couldn't prolong things or to allow the hope swelling inside her to grow any larger than it already had.

"Adelie," Maddox said in her wake, reaching the door first and opening it for her. "Thank you for this. If you—" He paused and then shook his head, letting his words trail off.

If she what? What was he about to say?

"Yes?"

He grimaced and turned his head away from her. "If you check your account, the money should be there by Friday."

A lump bulged in her stomach. Right. The money. That's what this was all about, after all.

"Thanks," she said. "I'll see you later."

She tore herself away and headed out to her car, chiding herself with every step for being so foolish. What had she been doing, imagining interest from him when there was none? He was only fascinated with her because of his park. No matter what, she had to remember that.

10

A delie propped the rake against her side and removed her phone from her pocket. It hadn't buzzed. It hadn't rung. Yet, the doggone thing kept summoning her to glance at it every five minutes, the way it had since she'd left Maddox Hatter's mansion six weeks ago.

"You need a hobby," Suzie said, raking dead leaves that hadn't been cleared last fall and had slumbered beneath the snow all winter long.

"And you need to get off your sister's case and let her do whatever she wants," Fletcher said, wrapping his arms from behind Suzie and planting a kiss on the side of her neck.

Suzie playfully pushed him aside, lobbing a glare that lasted no longer than a blink before she smiled.

"Thank you," Adelie said pointedly, looking directly at the adorable red-headed man who'd been enamored with her sister for the past four years. Why he hadn't proposed yet, Adelie didn't know. They seemed content with the snail's pace of their relationship, and if that was enough for them, it was enough for her too.

"I'm just saying you need something to keep you too busy to look at that dumb thing every second."

"I've been plenty busy," Adelie argued, thinking of all the work they'd been doing on the house since the money from Maddox had come through. She pocketed her phone again and resumed impaling the leaves and coercing them into the pile near the sidewalk in front of their vintage, country bungalow.

"Sure, busy on social media."

Adelie stopped raking again. "Is there a crime in wanting to check for updates?"

She'd been stalking Maddox and his Wonderland on Facebook for weeks, not to mention her message and email inboxes. She couldn't deny the prick of hurt at being ignored. They had a connection during the few days they'd spent together—or so she'd thought. The days had continued, however, and every day she muscled down her disappointment at not having heard a word from him.

She tried reasoning with herself. He was busy. He owned a theme park that was being entirely rebranded for goodness' sake. The arguments didn't completely quell her disappointment or the nagging fear that everything she'd felt between them had all been one-sided. Unrequited, like always.

Against her better judgment, she'd been entertaining more and more daydreams since the photo shoot. Daydreams of carousel rides and crooked smiles, of time in Maddox's company and the roller-coaster plunge her heart longed to take, straight smack into love.

Was this what it felt like to love someone? Adelie didn't know, but she craved to. She wanted to experience for herself how two random people managed to not only find one another, but overcome fears, take chances, and win one another's affections and loyalty.

Looking at love according to facts like that seemed so illogical, but the world was flooded with people who proved otherwise, and Adelie wanted to be next.

"I think the grass is saying, 'ow,'" Fletcher said.

"Huh?" Adelie blinked from the stupor of her thoughts to find a bare patch of dirt where fledgling, yellow-green spring grass used to be.

"You all right there?" Fletcher added, gripping the black garbage bag he'd been holding for Suzie to dump in her pile of litter mingled with dead leaves. Suzie glanced at her as well, concern in her forehead. She knew all too well what was on Adelie's mind.

Suzie deposited her pile into the sack, straightened, and used her wrist to brush her blonde hair away from her forehead. "Why don't you just call him?"

Adelie shook her head and started raking a different spot.

"It's totally normal to ask for an update on the images he took of you."

"Not to mention within your rights," Fletcher said. "It was part of your contract." Fletcher was good at wordy documents. Adelie was grateful she'd had him look the papers over before she met with Maddox during their tour.

Adelie traipsed to the nearby maple tree and used it for support. "I would feel so stupid," she said. "So obvious."

Fletcher frowned. "Obvious about what?"

Suzie rolled her eyes and shuffled forward a few steps. "You've got nothing to worry about," she said, "not if Maddox is as observant as this guy." She nudged a thumb in her boyfriend's direction.

Fletcher glanced between the sisters with a puzzled expression, and the girls laughed. He really was cute. Suzie had been crazy about him from the start, and so giddy the day she'd come home from class and announced she had a date with him.

Adelie had thought about calling Maddox more times than

she cared to admit. She'd stared at his name in her contacts, but she could never bring herself to tap it. Wonderland had been closed for two weeks now, which meant something had to be happening. He'd said he would call her when the images were ready. Why hadn't he?

She'd given up checking social media. In fact, even though she'd stalked every possible sight for an update, she'd avoided it for the past several days altogether in an attempt to eliminate some of her frustration.

Together, Fletcher, Suzie, and Adelie bagged the leaves and stray branches left over from Westville's most recent spring wind. The air was chilled but not cold. Sunlight burst through the clouds, bringing with it the promise of flowers and outdoor adventures. They hauled the bags out to the curb for the city to gather during its neighborhood cleanup that weekend, and Tyler Wilborn rode past on his bike, slowing down at the sight of them.

He had to be eleven or twelve years old, his dark hair tufting out over his forehead, his cheeks flushed with exertion.

"Hey, there, Addy." Tyler pulled his bike to a stop near the garbage can and scrubbed a hand beneath his nose.

"Hey, Tyler," Adelie said. She'd known every kid on these streets since she'd been a kid herself. It wasn't unusual for them to pull aside and talk to her. Kids never gave her the anxiety adults did.

"I saw your pictures. I hardly recognized you, but you look seriously great."

Adelie shot a glance at Suzie, but her sister had already whipped out her phone and scrolled greedily with a finger on the screen.

Suzie's eyes boggled. She held up the phone as if in reverence. "Oh. My. Goodness. Look at you!"

Fletcher peered over. "Whoa," he said. "That's Adelie?" His

gaze shot to her before returning to Suzie's phone. "You look amazing."

"Right?" Tyler said. "I've been showing all my friends. It's so cool that you're like, famous, and you live on my street."

Adelie's entire body tingled. A bowling ball sank into her stomach. She couldn't bring herself to look. She was too fazed by the fact that Maddox had already put them up. He'd posted the pictures, and he hadn't told her.

"Well, see ya," Tyler said, riding off.

Filled with determination, Adelie yanked her phone from its pocket, opened Facebook, and gaped. Notifications blazed red. She had at least a dozen friend requests from people she didn't even know. Others—lots of others—had tagged her in posts. News stations, newspapers, Wonderland's main page—even Maddox had tagged her from his personal page.

Though the air around her was cool and crisp, walls began to close in around her. She shook her head, voicing her denial.

"It can't be." She felt exposed, vulnerable, as though a target had been pegged to her back and everyone in the world was taking aim.

"Why?" she went on, asking no one in particular. "Why would he post them already?"

Why hadn't he told her first?

"Something wrong?" Fletcher asked, sidling in. His heat radiated to her, and she was grateful for his proximity. She needed someone close to her just then.

"He didn't tell me," she said.

"Was he supposed to? That wasn't in your contract."

Fletcher's words ignited something inside of her. "Doesn't courtesy have its own unspoken contract?"

Apparently not, she thought, answering her own question. Fuming, she trudged along the sidewalk leading to the separate garage and the makeshift garden shed Grandpa Carroll had built. While Adelie felt like flinging the rake against the wall, she placed it gently down and headed in through the back door.

The house's warmth seeped into her skin, but it didn't soothe her. Adelie kicked off her shoes in their mudroom with its new beadboard along the walls and hung her jacket on its peg. Her thoughts exploded like fireworks in her mind. She ran through her last conversation with Maddox after the photo shoot had ended. He'd said he would call her. He'd promised he would. So, what was the deal here?

A buzzing sound came from her pocket.

Adelie dug for it. Her fingers seemed to lose their ability to clamp onto objects, and the phone slipped and crashed to the floor.

"No," Adelie said with a little gasp. She dove, but it was too late. The screen read *Missed Call: Maddox Hatter*.

Adelie hugged the phone to her chest and slumped against the wall. She missed it. He finally called her, and she had to go and drop her phone.

Suzie peeked her head around the corner from the adjoined kitchen. "Was it Mr. Billionaire?"

Adelie stomped her foot. "He finally called, and I had to go and drop it."

"Call him back."

A brand-new crack streaked across her phone. Worried it would no longer work, she tested it with her finger and opened the call screen.

Tap.

"Adelie, hey."

Maddox's voice would have been the stuff of dreams, but she was too upset to notice.

"Hey," she replied, amazed at her ability to speak with her heart galloping as fast as it was.

"I'm glad you returned my call. I've got some good news—or

maybe you've seen already." Delight decorated his tone. He was happy about this? "The images are ready. In fact, they're in place now. We took the last several weeks getting everything set up—"

"You—you hung them up already?" Without showing her?

"They look absolutely remarkable. Seriously, you pulled this off with complete flair. The grand reopening is next week—"

She was still trying to process. Not only had the images been blasted all over social media, but they'd been hung up near the rides. She did sign a contract to give him permission to do what he wanted with the images. Still. He *should* have let her know.

"I'd love to have you join me. A news crew will be there; you can tell them all about your experience and—"

"No." The last thing she wanted was another interview. More cameras? He was already displaying everything. The least he could have done was tell her. Instead, he'd made it public and she was the last to know. She was always the last to know. Her eyes slammed closed.

"I—Adelie, are you sure? It'd be great to have you there."

Her jaw quivered. "No, thank you. I'll be busy that night." Busy hiding. Too late, she realized he hadn't even told her the date or time of the reopening. Her aversion was obvious, but then again, maybe he wouldn't get it. Maybe he was oblivious like Suzie joked about earlier.

"I'm sorry to hear that," he said. "Let me know if you change your mind."

"I will," she said, blinking away tears. She was ready to end the call. Ready to never speak with him again.

"I'll deposit the rest of your money," he added.

"Great. Thanks. Bye, Maddox." She hoped he read the finality in her tone. She'd been so stupid, indulging in her fantasies based on two measly afternoons spent in his company and thinking it meant something. She'd been hurt enough. She couldn't risk it again.

addox stared at his phone, trying to make sense of what had just happened. Here he'd expected her to be over-the-moon ecstatic, and she all but hung up on him. What was that about?

Things had been so hectic with the rushed timeframe his team had developed. He'd been distracted, approving each new idea and design for the rides. He had been trying to make the outrageous deadline with nothing but the end result in mind.

He'd considered showing Adelie sooner, but part of him wanted to present the finished product to her and see the light in her eyes when she witnessed herself as Alice.

He'd never expected her to decline. Not only that, but to pronounce herself busy? He hadn't even told her the date of the reopening.

Maddox had thrown out the reminder of the money, hoping to prolong the conversation or lead it in a new direction, to get her to open up to him again, but it had only seemed to bother her more. This was not going as he'd planned.

11

A week later, Adelie pushed the shopping cart along the produce section of Coleman's Grocery and stopped at a particularly juicy display of apples. Soon it would be summer, which was her favorite time of year for produce. Corn on the cob, prickly pineapples, cherry tomatoes, new potatoes, and grapes the color of plums.

She couldn't deny that having enough funds in her bank account to pay for food—without having to worry about where the money was going to come from—made shopping that much more satisfying. But having her pictures smeared all over the news and social media outlets made her queasy. She couldn't go anywhere without seeing her own face plastered on a billboard or a newspaper, and each new sighting stripped away another layer of whatever well-being she had left.

The resulting nervousness she had was outrageous. She hadn't been able to relax enough to sleep soundly since the images had surfaced, since Maddox had invited her to Wonderland's reopening. Anxiety made swiss cheese of her insides.

She occasionally managed to steady her breathing and find peace of mind enough to do her studies and finish the homework for her classes, but it would be frayed by a well-meaning neighbor's comment or a new tag on Facebook. She really needed to stay off social media.

Adelie knew people were only being kind or excited and trying to show their support, but every comment, every statement, made her feel that much more vulnerable. Celebrities dealt with this all the time, she told herself. They still juggled their careers with a semi-normal life.

But she was no celebrity. She was just her. Just plain and simple Adelie. She hadn't asked for this fame. Hadn't sought it out, which was probably the reason these thoughts never consoled her. She still felt as though the pictures had embedded some sort of tracking device inside her, that people were watching her everywhere she went, even as she slept.

If she could get away with it, Adelie would never leave her house again. Eventually, she would attempt to find a new job, maybe once she got her nursing degree. As it was, it wasn't until she and Suzie were completely out of food that Adelie convinced herself to venture out.

It was just the grocery store. Nothing would happen to her while she was at the store.

With the help of Maddox's investment, she'd been able to pay off a large majority of their mortgage. They'd fixed the plumbing. They'd redecorated. Adelie reminded herself of these facts on an hourly basis. It was okay. She'd get her groceries and go back home where she could hide and pretend the world was as small as it'd been a hundred years ago, before social media and billionaires who owned theme parks decided to try and expand her horizons.

Adelie picked through the pile of rosy apples, dropping a few in her bag, when movement caught her eye. A man rested a hand on the edge of a large display filled with lemons. But he wasn't selecting lemons.

His attention was fixed on her.

A shiver trailed down her spine. Adelie pivoted. Ordinarily, she took her time selecting fruit with the right amount of shine, free from bruises or spots. This time, she grabbed the first half dozen she encountered and stuffed them in her bag. Still sensing the man's gaze, she peered from her periphery.

Another man had joined the first. He wore an overlarge coat open to reveal a flat-tire midsection jutting out over his jeans. The first man caught her glance. He nudged his friend with an elbow before jutting his chin in her direction.

"Nice apples," he said.

The insinuation in his statement sickened her. Adelie's throat tightened. She turned away without replying and headed toward the bagged, prewashed lettuce.

Instinct flared, pricking the skin at the back of her neck. *Leave the lettuce,* a small voice warned. She ignored it, telling herself this was nothing. It was all in her head.

She glanced behind to find the same man closing in on her.

Fear settled in. She wanted to abandon her cart, race off, leave the store and the creeps, but her feet refused to move.

"Saw your picture. It's you, isn't it? *Alice.*" His front teeth were crooked. He said the word like a verdict.

She retreated a step and swallowed. "I don't know what you're talking about."

"This? This isn't you?" He held up his phone and displayed Maddox's favorite picture of her. The one he'd texted and told her she looked beautiful in.

Ritchie had implanted a mesmerizing forest instead of the green screen around her, and she glanced over her shoulder as she reached for the apple dangling from the tree. Even she could tell her expression was seductive and alluring—two words she never would have associated herself with. Her vision went red.

Panic clicked into her brain. These men weren't like the

other admirers she'd had, who only stopped to offer sweet compliments before moseying on their way. They zeroed in on her like predators to their prey, and the realization made her back arch like a cat's.

She glanced around, searching for an associate or someone who might help her, but aside from these men, she was alone in the produce section.

"I love the new look," the man with crooked teeth went on. "Makes me wonder what you're like on a more...personal basis. Are you as sweet as this?"

"Excuse me." Deserting her shopping cart, she turned on her heel and picked up the pace, heading for the exit. She struggled to remove her phone from its pocket. It caught on the fabric, refusing to come free. Too late, she realized she'd dropped her purse along the way as well.

Beyond the checkout aisles, the exit blared at her like a strobe light. The faster she went toward it, the faster the men followed. One of their hands brushed her elbow. Against her will, a cry of panic escaped.

"Hang on, there," one said. The men hurried around, blocking her path feet from the collection of shopping carts and a row of flowers and helium balloons waiting to be picked over and given as gifts.

Adelie lost her footing. She staggered and found herself caught from behind by a pair of hands.

"Let me go!" she cried, but fear choked the plea to something timid and weak. She wriggled and wrenched, but the accompanying voice cut through her fear with distinct familiarity.

"Adelie. It's me."

Her gaze shot up to find Maddox's concerned face and pale green eyes concentrating on her. She crumpled into him out of sheer relief. His warm arms encircled her, but they didn't dispel the dread pounding through her.

"Problem here, boys?" Maddox said. His voice rumbled in his chest.

Adelie whirled around to find the two men snarling at her, shoulders rising and falling, faces flushed. A crowd had also collected. Several shoppers slowed their carts to gape, several with phones in hand.

"I'm calling the police," Adelie said through her teeth.

"Already done," a woman behind the men said. Her hair was short-cropped and gray, but she held a no-nonsense expression in her fierce eyes. "I got their picture too." She held up her phone.

"Sounds like you boys better keep a low profile from now on," Maddox said with warning in his voice. His hand was firm against Adelie's back, securing her to him.

The men called out several expletives in Maddox and Adelie's direction before elbowing their way out of the surrounding crowd, past Maddox, and toward the exit.

It wasn't until they were gone that Adelie's entire body went limp. She slumped against Maddox's side, relieved at having him there. Tears sprang to her eyes, made all the starker by the sour tang in the back of her mouth.

"Are you okay?" Maddox asked, bending to meet her eyes. "Did you know either of those losers?"

"No," Adelie said, answering both of his questions with a single word. She clutched at her chest, her muscles tight and defensive. She was shaking. Who knows what those men would have done to her if Maddox hadn't shown up when he did?

He rubbed a hand in soothing motions up and down her arm. "It was all I could do to not take them both down right there. Guys like that are total creeps." He added a few additional, rougher explanations of what he'd like to do to men like them.

"I want to leave," Adelie said, unable to process his words. It was the only thing playing in her mind over and over. Leave. Escape.

"We will. But if that woman called the police, then you might want to give them your statement so they can keep an eye out for those douchebags."

It was as though a balloon had released its air. People converged, smothering Adelie with questions about her well-being and congratulating her for standing up to the creeps. Adelie could only shake her head. She didn't want to talk to anyone. She never wanted to set foot outside again.

"I'm fine," she said to no one and everyone as a police officer strode to where she and Maddox stood.

The dark-skinned officer, too young to be bald and yet with head shaven and a blunt goatee, approached with one hand on his belt. His car remained visible through Coleman's glass, automatic doors, its lights still flashing. Adelie recoiled. Nothing like bringing more attention to the scene.

Then again, she was grateful the officer was here, risking his own life for the safety of others, grateful Maddox remained by her side, rubbing calming circles on her back.

Adelie answered the officer's questions as best as she could. "I was minding my own business, trying to buy a few things we needed, and these men wouldn't stop following me. They patronized me, made lewd, suggestive comments, and then they started following me out of the store when I tried to leave."

"Adelie," Maddox said with such sympathy it dragged a few more tears from her eyes.

"I see," said the officer, asking for descriptions, for any further information she could give that might be of use. The older woman who'd spoken in her defense stepped forward to show the officers the picture she'd taken on her phone before wishing Adelie good luck and pushing her cart away.

The store manager interceded, offering to give the policeman a look at their security feed. Adelie and Maddox both explained the reasoning for the attention, that she'd recently become the face of Wonderland's new brand. The officer made his record and then offered his condolences.

"Call us immediately if anything like this happens again," he said. "And it sounds like you might want to hang tight until publicity dies down," the officer told her. He took a pause, walking away before turning back. "It might not be a bad idea to stay somewhere you feel safe for a while."

Somewhere safe? It wasn't as though she had miles of secure fences surrounding her house, or the luxury of a stern security guard to bar anyone's entrance. How had she ever been enamored with Maddox's house? With him, his lifestyle, with the money he'd given her?

Money. What a joke. Money was so not worth what she'd just gone through.

Adelie couldn't help but think of Alice in the story. Growing larger one second, then smaller the next, with nothing more than a drink from a strange bottle or a bite of mushroom. After the pictures had been posted, after seeing the reception they were receiving, having Maddox share what a success everything was (via text since she'd refused to answer any of his calls), and then writing a check to pay cash for her house, it was like Adelie had grown. Tripled her own size, or at least the size of her head.

But now this? She'd shrunken. Now she felt three inches high. She wished she could go back, erase everything. She wished she'd never gone to Wonderland with Suzie, that she'd never sat at that stupid tea party table, that she'd never muttered the riddle to it.

And then she went and agreed to do a photo shoot? To put her face all over town, all over the nation? What had she been thinking?

12

"Should have just followed my gut," she snarled, working her way from Maddox's side to retrieve her fallen purse and then back again toward the exit.

"Hey," he called after her. His footfalls thumped in her wake, and then he was at her side in the bright, mocking sunlight.

"Hey, are you sure you're okay?" He continued trudging beside her, keeping her rapid pace.

She paused, tossed and turned, so confused. Where had she parked? Why were there so many cars here?

"I—I don't know, Maddox," she said, not looking at him.

He gripped her wrist. She shook him off. He persisted. "Can I give you a ride home? I'll have Kirk pick your car up for you later."

She took him in for the first time since he'd come to her rescue. Maddox wore a cozy sweater with gray and tan stripes and jeans and looked far too appealing for the frustration simmering through her.

"Take it down," she demanded. "Take it all down."

He rotated, following her. "What are you talking about?"

Tears pooled in her eyes, rendering him a blur. She hadn't

been able to process it all, but now that her emotions had a chance to settle, the reality of everything tumbled around her. The confrontation was invoking too many suppressed feelings from her past, feelings she'd worked hard to let go of.

"I don't want it. I changed my mind."

Maddox put his arm around her shoulders. "Come on, come for a drive with me at least. I think we need to talk, and it sounds like you definitely need someone with you right now."

"What does that mean?" She shouldn't sound so defensive, but she couldn't help it. What was he implying? She already felt weak enough as it was; she didn't need him reminding her she'd almost been abducted and possibly molested or whatever horrid actions those men had in mind.

"I mean, I'm not about to leave you alone after what I just witnessed. Those guys were trouble. Please, let me give you a ride home. We can talk in my car and you won't have to worry about anyone overhearing."

A pair of teenage girls stood near Coleman's entrance, giggling and talking behind their hands. One of them called out, "Hey, Alice!"

Adelie closed her eyes. Wasn't there anywhere she could go without being seen?

"Okay," she said. She did want to talk to him away from prying eyes.

Together, they strolled to where he was parked. Maddox opened the passenger door to his Lexus and waited until she sat down before he closed it again.

Maddox headed for the freeway and they sped along down the road toward Manchester, weaving in and out of traffic. Though she wondered where he was taking her, she didn't care enough to voice it. Instead, she focused her attention on the scenic beauty surrounding them.

It was an unspoiled forest, interrupted by asphalt, and the

scenery was infectious, simplistic, and vibrant. She'd always loved living in Vermont because of the landscape alone. This was what had inspired Robert Frost to write such stunning words about nature, and she got to live here.

"Okay," he said. "I'm going to drive out to the Shires. That should give us plenty of time and privacy to talk. Is that okay?"

She'd roamed along the Shires several times with her church youth group growing up. It was a beautiful area with luscious trees, rocky streams, and several nice walking paths, and it was just the respite she needed.

"I'm so sorry this happened to you," he began. "Do you want to talk about it?"

"Not really," she said truthfully.

He inhaled through his nose. "Fair enough. I'll make good on your request, Adelie. I'll take everything down, all the pictures, the billboards, everything. I never anticipated that you'd get such negative attention, that you wouldn't be able to do something as simple as grocery shopping without hordes obsessing over you."

"I—yeah. It's kind of awful."

His ready offer to redact the new images affected her. She never expected him to actually agree. Maybe it was that fact that made her hesitate. To have him remove everything just like that? Sure, she'd demanded as much back at the store, but he'd already invested hundreds of thousands of dollars into this —into her.

"But what about your profits?"

"Your safety is more important than my profits."

The words sank into her like a drink of hot chocolate, soothing the chill that had been building inside. How could she let him do that? It hadn't been his fault the creeps had come after her.

The truth was, Maddox had offered her the chance of a lifetime, and she'd accepted it, risks and all. She just needed to learn how to deal with everything a little better than she had. And carry a can of pepper spray with her everywhere she went.

Even women who weren't famous got stalked by psychotic ne'er-do-wells. Learning a little self-defense might not hurt either.

"You put so much into this," she began as he took a right turn and slowed toward the stop sign at its end.

"Doesn't matter," Maddox stated emphatically.

"Yes, it does. Even if you take all the signs down, the social media exposure still has the images. There's no way to undo this, not really."

With the roadway clear, Maddox accelerated, spearing past several slower-moving cars on his way toward the breathtaking mountains that made up much of northern Vermont's landscape.

"I'm so sorry, Adelie. I feel like I have to do something to make it right."

"This isn't your fault." She startled herself with the veracity of her tone. Little by little, good things about this situation began to filter in, drip by drip, in a way they hadn't before.

It helped to be here with him now, to know she wasn't alone in this. She'd felt so lonely, as though she were treading on sinking stones and waiting for the fall. So much of her anxiety had been based on the not-knowing.

"Thanks for offering," she added as the road inclined and the meadow-like fields filled once more with trees. "But I'll be okay. A little scarred after today, I won't lie, but they don't have grocery pick-up for nothing." She tried chuckling, but it didn't have the effect she'd hoped for.

Concern still dominated Maddox's face. He scowled at the road, not responding to her attempt at playfulness.

"I'll just lay low," she said. "Like Officer Warner suggested."

"You can't hide for the rest of your life."

"Maybe Officer Warner was right. I'll just wait until the park's publicity with your reopening and all these recent changes die down."

Maddox slowed and changed lanes. "How exactly do you plan on doing that?"

"Never leave my house?" she joked. Hey, with Amazon, grocery pickup, and Suzie around, it was totally possible. It was a good thing she loved her home as much as she did.

Maddox took the next turn, which led to a wider pull-off for those wanting to stop and take in the view. He pulled onto the shoulder and frowned at a pair of trees that had tangled their trunks as though someone twisted them together.

"I have an idea," he said, drumming his thumb against the steering wheel, "but you're probably going to hate it."

"What's that?"

"Stay with me."

She shifted on the leather seat. "What?"

He angled his head, still staring out the dash. "I know it sounds ludicrous and completely mad, but why not? Come, stay at my house for a while. You could have your own room, your own section, if you want. There's plenty of space. And you'd be totally safe there. I mean, you've seen my security. Why not?"

Sure, go stay at the billionaire's house with secure fences and cause even more speculation once word leaked she was living with him.

"Publicity is bad enough as it is now," Adelie said. "How are people going to react when they hear I'm *living* with you? They might think something is going on between us." She dipped her chin, embarrassed at having to be so blunt but knowing it was necessary.

"What if there were?" His tone was a captured butterfly,

gentle and delicate, fluttering just enough to make itself known. "People move in together all the time."

Adelie's mouth fell open. Was he seriously saying what she thought he was?

A handful of arguments elbowed their way to the forefront of her mind, but only one took center stage. *Moving in* together meant they were in a relationship. It implied they were more involved than two casual friends should be.

She thought of Suzie and their neighbors. What would people think of her if she went and moved in with Maddox? Rumors would spread, whether they were true or not.

"*If* I were to ever do something like that, I would want to be married, Maddox." She swallowed, willing herself to continue. "I know a lot of people don't think it's important, but it is to me."

Gumption had overtaken her, but after all the events of the past several weeks, she needed to be more upfront, especially right now. Maybe if she had been, she wouldn't be in this predicament in the first place.

"Okay, then. We wouldn't call it moving in. We could call it protective custody."

Adelie's eyes slammed shut, and annoyance coursed through her. Changing the name of something didn't change what it was.

Call her old-fashioned, but if her grandparents ever heard she'd moved in with a man—a man she was insanely attracted to and had dreamed about on more than one occasion—they'd roll over in their graves. Not to mention God's opinion on the subject, which mattered to her.

Maddox's chest rose. His hands rested on his legs. He hadn't yet shut the ignition off, and his car rumbled beneath them. He rotated to face her more directly.

"Okay, then. What if you marry me?"

"*What*?" In the realm of responses she might have expected, a proposal was on a different continent. *Marry* Maddox Hatter? On a whim, just like that?

This time, Maddox shifted in his seat. "Hear me out," he said. "People would believe a marriage. Whatever rumors might surface about the two of us would be answered from the start. No speculation. You could live at my house for as long as you needed to, ease your way into the public eye with me, and then maybe in a year or so, when you're feeling ready to take on the world again, we can part ways."

She could see his reasoning. Marriage would allow her as much time as she needed to feel safe again. Something told Adelie it wouldn't be as easy as he claimed, though. If she did this, she'd never be able to avoid the public eye again.

Then again, even if she didn't, it was already too late for that. But at Maddox's side, as his wife, he could help her learn how to cope with it better than she was.

This was nuts. Completely insane.

Then why was the idea so tantalizing?

"You're willing to do that for me? You barely know me. What do you get out of it?"

"Why should I get anything out of it?" His tone sounded almost offended.

"I just mean, it doesn't seem fair to you. It feels almost like I'm taking advantage of you. You've already given me so much. How can I expect anything more?"

His lips tugged upward. "Adelie, I'm the reason your life turned upside down in the first place. This is the least I can do, believe me. I talked you into the photo shoot because I was selfish. I wanted you so badly, I didn't think of the consequences, and it put you in serious danger. At least let me make this right."

His phrase dangled like temptation between them. *I wanted you so badly.* Marriage was about more than just living in the same space. If they did this, she'd have to make certain parameters undoubtedly clear.

"So, we would actually get m-married? I would take your name?"

"Only if you wanted to," he said. "I'd have to draw up some paperwork."

"More paperwork?"

There was that smirk again. "As some legal issues will be involved if we decide to move forward with this, I'll need to make sure certain aspects of my life are...protected."

He wanted to make sure she didn't steal his money. Fair enough.

"And if there are any issues I should be aware of with you, those can also be addressed."

"What about physically?" she blurted.

To her surprise, a slight flush overtook his skin. A muscle jumped in his jaw. "No expectations there," he said, slicing the air between them with his hand. "It can be a marriage in name only, if you want."

Did she? This was so much, so fast. She'd never even kissed a guy, let alone...anything else.

"And when...when would this all happen?"

"Your safety is important to me," he said, picking at the threaded border of the console between them. "If I'm not mistaken, I know a place where we can get a marriage license and get hitched by tomorrow."

Her entire body trembled. Adrenaline coursed through her, making her more alert to every word he spoke. Married to Maddox by tomorrow. *Tomorrow.*

"You'd better not say Vegas," she said.

Maddox laughed so boisterously the sound heated her chest. His hand found hers and carefully, deliberately, he slid it beneath her palm, positioning it perfectly so he could weave his fingers through hers.

The touch spoke everything he didn't need to say aloud. He was serious about this. And he would wait for her to make a decision. The problem was, she didn't have a clue what to do.

13

"No way. Marriage? Are you both out of your minds?"

"Suzie, come on," Adelie said across the suitcase lying open atop her bed to where Suzie had perched. "I thought you'd be freaking out and telling me to go for it."

The freak out happened to be her older sister's typical response to impulsive situations like this.

Adelie hadn't been able to think of anything else during the entire, mostly silent, drive back to Coleman's. Maddox had taken her right to her car and even gone as far as following her home to make sure she made it safely, rather than calling Kirk to pick up her car and drive her himself.

"I'm all in," he'd assured her as he'd walked her to her door. "Just say the word, and we'll do this."

Adelie's mouth had been too dry to reply. She'd chewed her lip, thanked him again for his help, and gone inside and straight up to her room.

"Of *course*, I think you should go for it," Suzie said. "He said it's not permanent, right? You'd have your own wing in his mansion. You could finish your degree while living in the lap of luxury. Just don't forget about me while swimming in his room full of gold coins like Scrooge McDuck."

Adelie folded another shirt and laid it in the suitcase. "I don't know, Suz. It's so—marriage."

Suzie flung a hand in the air. "Pfft. Tons of people only see it as a piece of paper anyway. No big deal. Ella's doing it. You might as well, too."

Adelie went rigid inside. That was just it. For Ella and Hawk, their engagement was the real thing, prompted by true, resounding feelings of love for one another that had come over time. Adelie wanted her marriage to fit those criteria. She wanted it to matter.

She'd fantasized about her wedding since she was a young girl. Walking down the aisle toward the man she loved more than anyone else in the world. Declaring herself his and having a forever kind of love, the way her grandparents had.

To marry a man she barely knew, knowing their marriage had an expiration date?

"What?" Suzie asked. "You're staring at nothing like a major, internal debate is going on in there."

Adelie closed the suitcase lid and flopped onto the mattress, resting her hands on her stomach and staring at the ceiling. "It's just so sudden. I'll be at his house...alone with him."

"You mean you don't want to stay alone with the mad Hatter?"

"He's not mad," Adelie said, too quickly.

Suzie rolled onto her side and rested her head in her hand. "Then what's the problem? Too tempting for you? Secluded quarters with a handsome billionaire... Security sees what's on the outside, but probably not the inside. You guys would have the place to yourselves. And with that whole ring-on-your-finger scenario, there wouldn't be much in your way."

"Suzie!" Adelie couldn't remember ever shrieking like that in her life, but her cheeks were so hot they might as well have been sunburned.

"You do know that's what happens when two people get married, right? Please tell me I don't have to have 'the talk' with you."

Adelie covered her face with her hands and then whacked her sister with a pillow. "That is *not* why I'm going."

"But you can't say the possibility of getting to know him a little better hasn't crossed your mind."

"And if it has?"

"See? This is your chance, Adelie. You guys already had a connection at the photo shoot. You were gushing about it like a schoolgirl."

The prospect of anything like that with Maddox would be off-limits. It had to be. Adelie changed the subject. "What about you? I couldn't relax there, living at his house, knowing you're here all by yourself."

"I have my job and my life. Fletcher will come over in the evenings—he's practically here all the time anyway. Besides, someone needs to stay in Grandma and Grandpa Carroll's house. We just got the plumbing fixed. Who knows? Maybe I'll talk Fletcher into a marriage of convenience. Won't Ella love that? Three marriages all in a row. Jane Austen-style."

Adelie didn't laugh. She knew Suzie had been waiting for years for a proposal from him and wasn't likely to get one soon.

"You sure you'll be safe without me?"

"What can you do to protect me, sis?" Suzie's tone was too skeptical for Adelie's liking. "I'm the older one. It's not my face all over the place. No one ever noticed me before. They still don't now. It's totally fine."

"Well..." Adelie traced a finger along the quilt's stitching. Possibility seared through her, but she worked to keep it in check. She was *not* going there to be with Maddox. The whole marriage thing was just a façade, to help keep her safe.

She would be going to keep out of the public eye. She would complete her online schooling and wait for the publicity to settle.

Suzie gave her a knowing smile and squeezed her hand before rising from the bed and heading into the hall. Adelie reached for her phone and tapped Ella's number. Regardless of Suzie's joke about double and triple weddings, she needed to double-check.

"Hello?" Ella answered in her perky, bubbly way. She'd always been the positive, plucky type of person Adelie both admired and envied.

"Hey, it's Adelie. Do you have a minute?"

"Sure, what's up?"

Adelie spilled the whole situation—or the marriage part of things, anyway. She left out the fact that Maddox had made the offer out of guilt.

"It's just that, I know it's so rushed," Adelie said, "and you've been planning your wedding with Hawk for months now. I don't want to steal your limelight."

Ella giggled. "I never even thought of that! Of course, I want you to get married. If you're happy and you love the guy, go for it. Hawk and I wouldn't miss it for the world."

"You—you want to come?"

"Uh, yes! You were planning on inviting me, weren't you? And you know Grammy will want to know, and she'll probably make sure everyone on the Larsen side comes—"

"No," Adelie said too quickly. Her heart pranced within her chest.

This couldn't be a huge event. It was meant to be a temporary fix to what was becoming an increasingly problematic situation. Now it felt like Adelie was making things worse.

"Sorry. We want it to be small. After all the publicity my images have gotten, we want to make sure as few people know about it as possible."

She was beginning to wish she'd never mentioned it to Ella in the first place.

"I get that," Ella said. "No worries, cuz. You can count on me. I won't tell a soul."

Adelie breathed with relief. "Thank you."

"I'm happy for you," Ella added. "You deserve so much happiness. He'd better sprinkle it on you every chance he gets."

"I'm happy for you too," Adelie said, ending the call.

She wasn't sure why she'd gone to Ella in the first place. Looking back, considering how hush-hush they wanted to keep this, she probably shouldn't have said anything at all, but for some reason, she wanted someone else's input apart from Suzie's. Ella's enthusiastic support, Suzie's confidence in her decision, made every other argument Adelie pitched at herself fizzle.

She was really doing this.

Anticipation surged within her as she reached for her phone.

Here comes the bride, Adelie texted Maddox. *As you said, I'm in.*

Great. I'll feel more comfortable with that. I'll send Kirk to pick you up first thing tomorrow morning.

It was so anticlimactic. So formal. So devoid of oomph and fanfare. She'd wanted to be swept off her feet, to be dazzled by a ring and a down-on-one knee approach, with e. e. cummings recited for good measure.

Who was she kidding? Men weren't exactly lined up for her, not unless she counted those of the psychotic, stalking, poor personal hygiene variety.

Maddox was decent. Decent *and* gorgeous. And rich. She

would be safe with him, and right now, that mattered more than anything. Love could come later.

If it ever came at all.

"P lease tell me you're joking." Duncan had been lying on Maddox's couch, tossing a tennis ball into the air and catching it repeatedly. Hearing Maddox's news, however, made him drop the ball and sit straight up in three seconds flat.

"Should I be?" Maddox said.

Duncan shook his head, resting a hand on the cushions on either side of him. "The girl is stunning, but marrying her? You'd better have some serious paperwork drawn up for this. And have you even talked to Ruby?"

The sound of her name jolted Maddox. He hadn't thought of her since the park had opened. Realizing he hadn't thought of her in so long a stretch was a triumph indeed.

"Do I need to?"

Duncan's eyes narrowed. "You know Ruby better than anyone else. She wore your ring the last time you were idiot enough to propose. She may not handle this news well."

Maddox fought away the warning in his ribs and attempted to sound as unperturbed as he wanted to feel. "So?"

Duncan stood from the couch. "*So,* if you're trying to protect this girl, feeding her to Ruby may be more dangerous than anyone she could encounter on a random trip to the market."

"Ruby ended our engagement," Maddox argued. "Why would she even care that I'm getting married to someone else? It's not like she's going to lop off Adelie's head for this."

Duncan bent for the tennis ball, which had rolled several

feet away. "Are you so sure about that? I can just see her calling for a beheading now."

Maddox didn't like this turn of the conversation. "I'm done with Ruby," he insisted. "I have been for years now."

Except he'd never managed to get the engagement ring from her. Ruby had said she wanted to keep it as a memento.

"Of all the good times," Ruby had added before tiptoeing up to give him a kiss that hadn't seemed like an ending at all. That kiss had done it. It had made him realize what a fool, what a puppet on her strings, he'd been. She'd played him even as she'd been breaking up with him.

Sure, she'd known he wasn't hard-up for cash, but any decent person would have returned the ring so he could at least get his money back. But no. She'd kept it, so it could sit in a drawer or in her jewelry box, gathering dust. Maddox vowed then and there that he was done with her, done with a woman who cared more about her own interests than anyone else's.

He was still done with her now. "Are you coming to the wedding or not?" Maddox asked. "I need a best man."

"Not at City Hall, you don't," Duncan argued, tossing the tennis ball once more and catching it. "But sure, man. If you want me there, I'll be there."

Relief stole over Maddox. He didn't really need a best man, but he did want his friend to be there. He'd be meeting Adelie in a few hours. Martha, his maid, had worked hard to prepare Adelie's room and what would become her private accommodations in his house. Maddox had gotten security codes and keys updated for her so she could come and go as she wanted as soon as she was ready to.

This would work out, he told himself, trying not to be thrown by the fact that in less than twenty-four hours he'd have a wife who was practically a stranger to him. A beautiful, adorable stranger.

This was for her. He'd meant it when he'd said as much. But he couldn't deny the pull she'd had on him from day one.

"It's nothing," he told himself once Duncan left. She'd be there under his protection, that was all. She was so shy, so insecure. He couldn't do anything that might push her too far or hurt her feelings. Not to mention his own failed engagement with Ruby. Keeping as much distance as possible would be the best option, for both of their sakes.

14

F letcher pulled up outside Westville's City Center building. Though Maddox had offered to have Kirk pick her up, she'd asked Suzie and Fletcher to take her instead. It made things seem a little less daunting that way.

A sign on a low barrier announced the building's name. The opening was dotted with flags, flowers, and squat bushes. Statues of men and women in suits added a finishing touch to the building's archway just before its entrance. The last time Adelie had been here was to vote. Now she was here to sign a certificate and marry Maddox Hatter.

It all seemed so extreme, but she didn't want to be living under the same roof with a man she wasn't married to, and she was very much looking forward to the security guards and tall fences surrounding his house's perimeter.

This won't last, she told herself, gripping the bouquet of daisies Suzie had gotten for her—from Coleman's of all places. She'd been repeating the phrase in her mind since she'd left home with Suzie and Fletcher. Odd, that the man who'd enabled her to save her family home was also the reason she had to leave it.

Suzie rotated from her place in the front seat. "Ready to get hitched?"

Adelie gripped the daisies' stems tighter. "You say that like it's easy."

"Because it is," said Suzie. "You don't love the guy. You don't owe him anything. You're doing this because he owes *you*."

Adelie couldn't completely agree. She'd meant what she'd told him in the car the day before. She didn't want to seem like she was taking advantage of Maddox. He'd already given her outrageous amounts of money.

"You'll be fine," Suzie said.

Adelie was tired of hearing that. Sure, she would be fine. She would have courage. This was her decision, and she was taking this chance.

She'd talked it over with Maddox, and while they could have both worn sweats if they wanted (yoga pants, in Adelie's case), they agreed to wear their Sunday best.

She'd sorted through her closet before throwing in the towel, however. This was her *wedding*. Brief in duration or not, it might be the only wedding she ever had, and she wasn't about to wear any ordinary dress.

She wanted a wedding dress.

Yesterday afternoon, she'd dragged Suzie with her to Darnell's, the best—and only—wedding store in town, and found the perfect thing. It was A-line with three-quarter sleeves, a floor-length, tulle skirt, and a delicate spray of embroidered flowers on the bodice, as though she'd romped through a meadow, plucked a sprig of wildflowers, and tucked them into the belt of white ribbon at her waist.

Suzie had helped her twine her blonde hair into knots at the base of her neck. If nothing else, she felt beautiful, and that was all she could ask for, under the circumstances.

"Ready?" Suzie said again, stepping out of the car and opening Adelie's door for her.

Adelie joined her outside. The sky could swallow her, it was so wide and blue and completely cloudless. Where her nerves had been frazzled during the photo shoot—and during every split second afterward—the most peculiar sense of calm settled over her.

She looked into Suzie's blue eyes. "Yes."

The single syllable word held so much more than its usual capacity. She *was* ready. She wanted this. Even stranger, it felt right in a way she couldn't explain. Impulsive, rushed, necessary, obligatory. But *right.*

Fletcher met the sisters and offered Adelie his arm. Grateful, she took it, sliding her other arm through Suzie's. Together, they entered City Hall to find Maddox waiting with their marriage license in hand.

Duncan Hawthorne stood at his side, looking dashing in a suit of his own, but she only had eyes for Maddox. He wore a navy suit the color of dark seas and midnight stargazing, set off by a dark shirt and black tie. Her heart skipped a beat. She cradled the daisies to her chest and chewed her lip, completely entranced by him.

His lips parted, and the most delicious gleam ignited in his eyes, which never left hers.

"You look like a bohemian goddess," he said.

Adelie dipped her chin. "You look pretty good yourself."

Maddox visibly swallowed before holding the marriage certificate toward her. "Just need your signature," he said. "And then we can—"

"Get married?" Adelie finished.

He cleared his throat. "Yeah."

"Steady now," Duncan muttered under his breath.

As a matter of fact, Adelie's hand *was* steady as she took the certificate to the nearby counter, borrowed a pen from the adjacent cup, and signed her name. She paused only at the sight of Maddox's messy signature on its own line above hers.

Just how far would they take this marriage? Would she change her name? Adelie Hatter had a ring of dizziness to it.

A man approached and introduced himself as the deputy marriage commissioner. He shook Adelie's hand first and then Maddox's.

"You two ready to tie the knot?" he asked.

"We are," Maddox said.

The commissioner inclined his head. "Okay then. Our private ceremony room is just down here."

Adelie moved in a daze. She stood on one side of the polished desk within the small room, with Suzie and Fletcher behind her. Maddox stood across from her, with Duncan at his elbow. Out of the corner of her eye, she saw Ella and Hawk slip in, settling themselves in the seats behind Suzie and Fletcher.

Vows were spoken. Promises were made. Before she knew it, the final, token words pronounced them man and wife.

"A kiss is customary," the commissioner said, "though not necessary."

A kiss. Her entire body seized. She'd imagined this moment so many times. Wondering how it all worked, how a man's lips managed to find just the right spot on her own.

She'd read of thousands of kisses, of stymying moments perfectly crafted to make the readers' hearts flutter. She'd witnessed kisses in movies, thrilling over the moment when the two romantic interests finally gave in to their budding attraction and defied whatever odds were against them, declaring their devotion with a single, mouth-meeting gesture.

Now it was her turn. It was finally time for her to experience the same thing, to feel her own flutter, to be utterly and completely taken by Maddox's lips pressing to hers.

Her heart raced. Her gaze was plastered to his. She could hardly breathe after all that had just happened. All that was about to happen.

Keeping his eyes on hers, Maddox lifted her hand to his lips. The touch of his mouth on her skin was a monument, a shrine, worthy of wonder and reverence. Her entire body tingled. If a kiss on her hand held that much effect over her, she could only imagine what it would be like when their lips connected.

But Maddox didn't follow the prelude of that kiss on her hand with an actual one to seal their marriage. The anticipation floating in her chest lost its momentum as, instead, he smiled at her, gave her a brief nod, and tucked the hand he'd kissed under his arm before turning to greet their few witnesses.

Mortification blazed in Adelie's cheeks. She stared at a spot on the floor, the easiest solution whenever she felt out of place.

"Thank you all for coming," Maddox said in response to the polite applause resounding in the room. He shook the commissioner's hand, waiting as Suzie and Duncan signed their names on the certificate as witnesses. After hugging her sister and Fletcher goodbye, Adelie strolled out of the room in a sea of doubt.

What was that? She'd thought he'd been impressed by her. She felt the attraction building between them as he'd clapped eyes on her. He'd called her a goddess. She was his *wife*. Why, then, hadn't he kissed her?

15

Adelie mulled through the ceremony for the entire drive from downtown Westville to its outskirts where Maddox's house was. This was only temporary, she told herself. It was only to protect her. He'd promised no physical expectations on his part. Still, the reminders didn't help soothe the sting of rejection. He hadn't kissed her.

She'd thought their connection was genuine. His attentiveness and comforting words during the photo shoot. The electric tension that had sizzled between them on the carousel. But he hadn't kept the promise he'd made, to tell her when the pictures were ready, and now this.

Why would he put his entire life on hold for her if he didn't have even a small bit of attraction toward her?

Guilt. The only plausible answer she could come up with was guilt. He was a nice guy who'd put her in danger inadvertently, and he wanted to assuage his own feelings. Either that or this was another ploy to garner publicity for his park, but Adelie pushed that suspicion aside. He couldn't be that heartless.

Though he sat beside her on the back seat of the limo, she couldn't bring herself to look at him or risk welcoming any kind of conversation right now. What would she say, *thanks for marrying me?*

The drive didn't take long and yet took eons all at the same time. Her own sense of regret began forming like a newly growing seed inside her, but she did her best to cast it aside.

Kirk didn't pull into the front of Maddox's estate, as she had the one and only time she'd been here, but instead deviated around the back, to where a series of large garage doors awaited. *Six garages? What did any one person need with that many garages?*

The farthest one opened, and as Kirk pulled in, Adelie's question was answered.

Cars in every make and model spread out around the garage space. Lamborghini, Ferrari, the Lexus she'd seen Maddox drive.

"Don't mind my collection," Maddox said, jerking her attention. It was the first words he'd spoken since they'd moved Adelie's suitcases to the limousine and settled into the spacious backseat with her.

He hasn't broken any promises, she reminded herself, shaking away the sting of rejection from their ceremony. *He said he would marry you, and he did. That's that.*

"They're really impressive," she said. "You seriously own all of these?"

"I do. Just little rewards I've granted to myself. This one was from when my mom first approved my idea. This one was after the park opened." He rested a hand on the hood of a fancy Mustang.

"You're like Tony Stark," she said.

He shrugged. "Just without the insane brains."

"You're not insane?"

His lips quirked upward. He'd tugged his tie loose and undone the buttons on his collar, exposing the skin at his throat. "I never said that. Just that Tony Stark's level of intelligence far outweighs mine."

"Then you're not an industrial engineer."

"I'll tell you what I am."

She froze, either from the tone or the insinuation buried within it. "What?"

"Hungry."

Adelie laughed, crackling through her own tension, and took his outstretched hand.

Her fingers slid through his with the force of a shock. His soft skin sent sizzles up her arm and to her spine. It was made more intense when he closed his hand around hers and walked alongside her through the lavish columned hallway and into an expansive kitchen.

He hadn't kissed her, but he was holding her hand. Maybe he wanted to take things slow. Her respect for him took things up another notch.

A woman stood at the stove, wearing an apron and retrieving a pan of steaming biscuits from within. Something tantalizing was cooking in a pan, and she set the pan down in time to retrieve a wooden spoon and stir.

"That smells amazing," Adelie said.

"It's all Martha's doing. Adelie, this is Martha, my cook and housekeeper. She'll be here throughout the day, cleaning up and straightening whatever messes you make."

The smirk on his face told her he was joking. He'd been this way the first time she'd met him too, at the tea party table. Blurting things to make her wonder if he was really serious. This is not at all what she would have guessed a billionaire would be like.

"I'm not messy."

"Don't mind him," Martha said. "I never believe a word he says anyway."

"When have I ever lied to you?" Maddox faked defensiveness.

Martha dished the biscuits onto a porcelain platter and bustled them to the table. She directed her answer to Adelie rather than her boss. "This guy told me you two were getting married today."

"We did," Maddox said.

Martha planted a hand on her hip. "Then where's the lady's ring, hmm?"

Adelie dipped her chin to her chest, embarrassed. Yet another reminder that this marriage was anything but conventional.

When he didn't answer, Martha nodded and returned to retrieve the roasting pan from within the kitchen's second oven.

To his credit, a flush of pink colored his cheeks as well. He sidled in. "Would you like to change before dinner?"

Adelie glanced down at her dress. "That would be nice."

Truth be told, she wasn't sure she'd want to come out again once she'd changed into something more comfortable. It'd been a long day, and she was feeling beyond exhausted.

Kirk trailed in, passing them with her suitcases in hand. Maddox feigned surprise and lifted a hand in the direction Kirk had taken.

"Right this way, then," he said.

Adelie followed Maddox to the hall. Her room was farther than she'd thought it would be. It took several twists and turns before Maddox inclined two steps and opened the door into the most amazing chamber she'd ever seen.

"I had this prepared for you. I wasn't sure what you liked, but I know you like books, so I had some brought in." He gestured to her own personal reading nook, complete with wide windows and a cushioned bench.

"Oh, my goodness."

"And over here, this is where you can put your computer when you need to do your homework for classes."

He pointed out a desk that overlooked a gorgeous expanse of lawn outside.

"And this is my favorite part." He pushed open the double doors and stepped out onto the balcony.

A balcony. She had. A balcony.

"I'm in serious trouble," she said, striding out into the cooling air and gazing at the surroundings that were becoming more surreal by the minute.

"Why is that?" he said.

She could sense the heat roiling from him, the energy. It mirrored her own desire to step closer, to be held in his arms. *He* was trouble, that was for sure. Her sister's words drifted through her mind, about seclusion with him. That wasn't why she was here.

She moved toward the ledge. "Because you're spoiling me. I'm never going to want to leave."

"Maybe you won't have to," he said.

Brow furrowed, she turned to face him again. "Come on. You can't mean you want me to pack it in and move here."

"Why not? Cozy. Comfortable. Secure."

"Maddox, you really are crazy," she said, laughing and turning toward the view once more.

"Crazy enough." His low, alluring voice caressed her. It was closer than it'd been before. She caught a glimpse of him through her periphery. He stood right behind her.

Adelie closed her eyes, listening to him breathe. Energy seeped from him, and the heat of his proximity drove her mad. She waited, aching for his hands to seek her waist, to pull her closer to him, to cradle her to his chest.

How she longed to be held by him, to hear his heartbeat, to feel his body against hers.

He cleared his throat. "If you're not busy right now, would you like to see the best part of my home?"

Tentative and slow, she faced him. She'd been right—he had moved closer to her. And he didn't step away as she'd turned. Only inches separated them.

"Better than this?"

His hand found hers again, so easily, so naturally, the way he'd done in the garage. His thumb stroked her skin. All at once, thoughts of changing into something more comfortable fled. Nothing was more comfortable than this. Comfortable and yet agonizing at once.

Fleetingly, his gaze flicked to her lips. She swallowed. Tilted in.

He didn't miss her cue. His lids half-closed. The moment encapsulated them, filling with emotions and pulsing possibilities. Adelie tingled, waiting, wanting, not daring to take the first step.

Maddox took it, but in the wrong direction. He backed away with a smile, though he kept her hand in his. "Trust me. So much better. But you might want to grab a jacket."

Adelie swallowed a bucketful of air. What was her problem? She was taking this marriage thing way too seriously.

She attempted to realign the havoc he'd wreaked on her thoughts, her entire being. "You mean now? What about dinner? And my dress?" She tugged at its skirt.

Martha seemed to be working hard out there, and from the smell of things, the food was close to being ready.

"We'll eat. She'd be put out if we didn't," he said with a wink. "Hurry and change. I'll meet you when you're ready." And with that, he stepped out and closed the door behind him.

16

Adelie met Maddox in the kitchen, which Martha had already cleaned up to shine brighter than chrome. A sumptuous meal was spread on the white tablecloth, and the settings rivaled that from the most intricate photographed images in a food magazine. The food was delicious—better than restaurant-quality, in Adelie's opinion. Then again, she didn't eat out all that much, and when she did, it was of the fast-food variety.

She savored every bite. Once they finished, Maddox set his napkin on the table. He was in a lightweight jacket and looking amazingly tempting. "Let's go," he said.

Rising to her feet, she slipped her hoodie on over her head. "Where are we going?"

"For a walk," he said.

He guided her out onto a decadent, stone balcony and took a meandering staircase that angled one way, then another, before finally descending to the pathway. To the left was a tennis court. The right, a basketball court.

"Do you play?" he asked.

"Not really. I've never been sports-y."

"Me neither."

"What?"

He nudged her with his elbow. "I'm kidding. We might have to come out and shoot some hoops one of these days. You might like tennis."

"I like watching affluent people play tennis," she corrected. "I'll kick back and watch you." Something told her she wouldn't mind watching him do pretty much anything.

"Here. This way." He gestured to the graveled path between rows and rows of trimmed hedges set off by flowerbeds springing with daffodils and tulips. A small lake lay to the right beside what appeared to be a pavilion.

"This almost feels like we're on our way to meet the Red Queen."

"I had my gardener copy traditional English gardens," he said. "Since I didn't want to include this in my park, I made it a special thing here. But this isn't the real treat. It's what's at the pavilion at the end of the garden that I want to show you."

Maddox walked alongside her, keeping so close he may as well have put his arm around her. At one point, she felt something at the small of her back. He was keeping her close, and regardless of the rejection she'd felt earlier, first at their wedding and again on the balcony, she found she didn't mind.

She felt safe with him. Safe here on his grounds, surrounded by his security, being fed by his housekeeper. This was a literal dream, just like the one Alice had toppled into.

The forest cascaded all around them. She was reminded of the Cheshire Cat, popping in and out on branches, and she half expected Maddox to have something like that rigged through the path.

The cover of trees blocked out the pastel swirls in the sunset. Soon, the path ended, and their footsteps were soft along the grass carpet.

"So," Adelie began. "Your name. Is that something I should start calling myself as well?"

"Why do you sound so skeptical about it?"

"I don't know how far we're taking this scenario." She waved her hand between them. For a minute, the only sound between them was their feet on the grass as they neared the pavilion beside the pond.

"I think it could be a good omen for us," he finally said.

Her brows pinched. "A good omen? How so?"

"Oddly enough, my last name was probably the reason my parents fell in love. Or my mom anyway. Like that Oscar Wilde play, *The Importance of Being Earnest*? For her, it was *The Importance of Being Hatter*."

Adelie laughed. "She named you Maddox Hatter, knowing exactly how it would make you sound?"

"You know, it's not that strange."

Considering what some celebrities named their kids these days, she supposed he was right. She couldn't ignore the implication of his comment, though. His name being romantic and the reason his parents had fallen in love was a good omen for them? Was he saying he was hoping they would fall in love as well? Adelie couldn't bring herself to ask.

"And Wonderland was your idea, or your mom's?"

He indicated a small path to the left, though it seemed there were several they could take. Curiosity itched within her to explore the other two paths, but she took the direction he indicated.

"The theme park was hers," he said. "She always envisioned a Wonderland of her own to wander through and pictured having rides there. I did my best to recreate it for her before she died."

"That's really sweet of you."

"This, though. I didn't want this in the park. I kept this part of things closer to home." He gestured to the glassed-over pavilion sprouting from within the cover of trees. It was so well hidden, Adelie guessed even something flying overhead wouldn't detect it was there.

"What is this?"

"Come on." He reached the door first and, using a key from within his pocket, unlocked it.

He waited, allowing her to enter first. Light gradually filled the space, whether by a sensor at her entrance or triggered by Maddox somehow, she wasn't sure. At this point, though, she was too struck by the surrounding artifacts to care.

"What is all this?" she asked, treading along cleverly constructed displays. It seemed to be his own personal museum. A mannequin stood in the corner wearing an antique dress. Collectible items. A single shelf housing a single book.

"My mom's," he said. "I told you, she was a fanatic."

Adelie circled in place. "This was her collection?"

Maddox trotted over to stand beside the mannequin. He ran a hand along the skirt. "Yeah, she'd collected this stuff since she was a kid. This dress was worn by an actress who portrayed Alice in a movie from the 1940s. I nearly had you wear it, but I couldn't bring myself to take it out of here."

"I'm glad you didn't," Adelie said. "I'd hate to be responsible for ruining it." She meandered toward the shelf. The book's old cover was brown and tattered. Its title was embossed on the spine. *Alice's Adventures in Wonderland.*

Adelie's breath caught. "Oh, my goodness, is that what I think it is?"

"Signed by Lewis Carroll himself," Maddox said, crossing the small area to join her. "Don't ask me where she got it from."

Adelie wanted to hug it. She loved books, but this wasn't just any book. It was the *original.* Other books joined it, though they looked like math books.

"This is so incredible," she said, circling to take in the other objects. A pair of white, kid gloves. A pocket watch. A set of teacups sat on white, braided display stands.

"How did you get all of these?"

"Again, I'm not entirely sure. These were all things we found, intricately labeled, within Mom's house after she'd passed away."

"I'm sorry she's gone," Adelie said, resting a hand on his wrist.

He glanced around his miniature museum. "Me too."

"Did she ever get to see this? All of this? Everything you did for her?"

"She saw Wonderland, but not like it is today. It was smaller then."

"You—" she began, so touched by his thoughtful, outlandish gesture and homage to his love for his mother.

"Me?"

"I don't even know what to say." How could she tell him how soft her heart felt in that moment, how drawn to him she was, seeing his tenderness and such care? How, resting his weight on the antique cane the way he was, all he lacked was a top hat and he would fit the part completely?

His gaze flicked to her lips. She cleared her throat and stepped back.

"How's the rabbit?" Adelie tucked her hair behind her ears. "I've thought about him and that traumatic day he had."

"He's in here, actually." Maddox returned the cane to its canister and opened the door to his left. Again, lights flickered on as though by a sensor. Adelie kept close to his side.

The air filled with the scent of animals, wood shavings, and feed. Several feet down, like a lost relic in a tomb, was a huge rabbit cage. Movement caught her eye. It was the twitch of long white ears.

She hurried her pace and hooked a finger through the cage's bars. "Oh, there he is."

Pierre froze in place, staring back at her with beady, red eyes. He'd been well taken care of in here, that was clear. His cage looked clean, his water tube filled, and plenty of food filled a dish linked onto the cage's side.

"He's so cute," she said.

"I knew it would be you, you know." Maddox spoke in that strange way of not sticking to the topic, or of leaping from one topic to the next.

Adelie straightened and faced him. "What?"

He sauntered closer, resting a hand on top of the cage. The lines of muscle on his arm became that much more evident. "The moment I saw you sitting there, looking totally content as the only guest at a mad tea party, I thought, wouldn't it be awesome if she was the one to find him? And you did."

"I—" Words failed her, stolen by the admiration gleaming in his gaze. No man had ever looked at her like that. Like she was special. Like she'd humored him, and he wanted her to keep doing it.

He shifted. "Did you figure it out yet?"

Her mouth was dry. So dry. She swallowed. "Figure what out?"

"Why a raven is like a writing desk?"

Adelie's heart was the rabbit in a cage. It pounded, trapped but not against its will. This was a willing entrapment, and it pulsed with the desire to remain a prisoner.

"That might be you," she said.

"Me?"

"The answer. To the riddle."

The corner of his lips quirked up. "Explain?"

She stepped away, needing distance. She couldn't handle a

third almost-kiss moment today, not unless he was going to *actually* kiss her.

"You're this billionaire, with a massive house. But that has nothing to do with who you really are. While anyone might think you started your livelihood as a ploy to get money, you did it for exactly the opposite.

"It's in honor of your mother and it just ended up being amazing because you deserve for it to be that way. Like the raven is nothing like a writing desk. You're nothing like what you make people think you are."

She wasn't sure if that made any sense.

"Adelie," he said, ending there as if saying her name was enough of a response. "How can you think I'm like the writing desk?"

She laughed and punched his shoulder.

He captured her hand and stared at it, rubbing his thumb across her skin. "You're wrong, you know. I am doing this for money."

The admission was a bee sting. Small, but sharp. She pulled her hand away. "I don't believe you."

"Well, maybe Wonderland wasn't about money to begin with, but it is now. I'm greedy. I'm not as wonderful as you seem to think."

"What if you're just as wonderful as I think?"

His gaze trailed from her hairline to her mouth, stopping when it met her eyes. "You've had a long day. Come on, I'll walk you back to the house."

He didn't deny his greed, and she couldn't help wondering the entire way back to his house what he'd possibly meant by admitting as much. Had their marriage been as she'd thought after all? He'd only done this for his own benefit?

She didn't want to believe it, but what else could she think?

17

Adelie rose from the bed and carefully arranged the blankets the best she could. She'd never been one to make her bed religiously, the way her grandma had, but she felt the responsibility now, in this house that was more like a palace. A place of luxury that demanded to be treated differently. She cared about the home she'd grown up in, but it was different from this somehow.

How would it be if she left the blankets disheveled? If she scattered her clothes across the floor? It didn't fit the space. She knew Martha would probably be along to make the bed or put up her clothes for her regardless, but Adelie didn't want to do that either. She had too much respect for herself, she supposed, especially after Maddox's comment to the maid the day before.

She crept toward the closet with its double-doored entrance and used two hands to throw them both open. The amount of space within the white closet took her breath away.

"This is bigger than my room."

She stepped in and swept an inquisitive gaze across the shelves. Some were thin and closer together—for shoes, Adelie suspected. Some were wide and tall, perfect for boxes or crates.

There were pegs to hang purses, beams for hanging shirts, and it was all vacant, all waiting to be filled.

Adelie hugged herself and plunked onto the rotund stool within the center of the closet. "I don't think I even have enough to fill a quarter of this."

She supposed she could bring her suitcases in here and begin to test her theory, but she dressed quickly in a simple pair of jeans and a pink t-shirt and then returned her pajamas to the suitcase. She brushed her teeth and hair, and stood, a stranger in a decadent room.

Logically, she knew this was now her home, for as long as she wanted it to be. Maddox had promised. But she couldn't trust the situation enough to settle in fully just yet. After the confusing end to their conversation the night before, she still worried he would pull the proverbial rug from beneath her.

This couldn't *really* be her home. She was a project to him, nothing more. He would grow tired of her. He'd back out on his promise. It was what her parents had done when they'd abandoned her. The only people she'd been able to rely on were her grandparents and Suzie. She had to remember that.

Sunlight splashed through the windows that made a hexagon shape around her. It was almost like an embrace, with the light pooling around her, the way the windows seemed to envelop her. Adelie wanted to allow it to sink in, to make her feel warmer in the space that was supposedly hers.

She'd accepted the money he'd offered for the photo shoot. She could accept her new position. But being his wife? Adelie didn't have any idea how to handle that, especially since he'd made it clear their relationship wasn't going to have any more closeness than what they already had.

It was okay with her. She just had no clue how to behave, if she were being honest with herself.

Adelie decided to act the way she would if she were at her

own house, and that meant opening her laptop and getting caught up on the schoolwork she'd missed the past few days.

Settling in at the desk near the window, she pulled up her online medical terminology course. Her teacher had posted an updated list of prefixes and suffixes which she needed to apply to memory if she had any chance at passing the next test.

It wasn't only that, though. She wanted to learn these terms. She wanted to be as fluent in the medical lingo as she could be in order to do her best during surgeries or whatever else she would help with during her nursing career. It wasn't like she could stop mid-surgery to consult her medical dictionary.

She hadn't checked the site since before her wedding and regretted it. So many terms waited for her to master them. It was so like learning a foreign language, it wasn't funny.

Adelie thought of her multiple attempts to learn French. Each time had failed, but this, she wanted to get this right. It would do her no good being a nurse if she didn't have a full grasp of the terms others around her would use.

Kicking back in her chair, she dove in. Catching up would be easy in a cozy corner like this. She wrote each component multiple times on a piece of paper. She took the preparatory quizzes online; she tested her own knowledge in as many ways as she could think of when a knock came on her door.

The cast of sunlight was in a different position, nearing closer to her pillow rather than at the foot of the bed where it'd been before. Stomach grumbling, she saved her progress, closed the lid on her laptop, and rose to answer it.

She really should have gone out for breakfast. A quick check on her phone told her it was closer to lunchtime now.

Maddox stood in the hallway, wearing a t-shirt that broadcasted a small Vermont town, and jeans. The casual look was good on him. His hair was swept from his forehead in an untroubled sort of way. He rested a hand on the doorframe.

"Hey, stranger," he said.

She slumped against the door's edge. "Hey."

They were married now. This man standing at her doorway? He was her husband. Adelie still couldn't quite believe it.

"I haven't seen you all day," he said. "Did you come out for breakfast?"

She rested a hand on her stomach while a pang of guilt struck her. Had he been waiting for her? Maybe they should clarify expectations.

"I—no, I didn't. I've been studying."

He nodded his understanding. Martha passed behind him in the hall, raising a single brow, her arms full of folded sheets. Maddox inclined his head in her direction.

Adelie fought an embarrassed smile. She wasn't sure why the maid seeing them in the doorway would bring heat to her cheeks, but she lowered her chin.

Adelie wondered if Martha was wondering why they weren't sharing a room. How much of their situation had Maddox told his staff?

He rubbed a hand behind his neck. "Mind if I come in?"

Her stomach sizzled at the thought. For all intents and purposes, this was her room. He would be entering her space, a place where they could shut the door and have complete and total privacy.

"Sure." She stepped aside and sank onto the bed, tucking a foot beneath her. Play it casual. "What have you been up to?"

"Working," he said. "Duncan is managing his new investments in Wonderland and he's been reaching out to several other investors as well. Things are looking to spike, thanks to you."

Adelie tucked a hair behind her ear. "It wasn't only me."

"I disagree, but that's beside the point." He gestured to the desk before padding toward it and running a finger along her laptop. "How's your studying going? What are you studying, anyway?"

"Nursing," Adelie said. "I want to be like the nurses my grandma had. They were living, breathing angels for her while she was spending so much time in the hospital."

"Your grandma was in the hospital?"

"Yeah, she had a stroke. It incapacitated her entire left side, and she kind of went downhill from there." Her throat closed. She wasn't used to talking about Grandma Carroll's last days with people who hadn't already been there to experience them with her.

"How long ago did she pass away?" Maddox's tone was sympathetic and kind. He had told her about his mom, after all. She appreciated his attentiveness about this.

"Six years ago. I'd recently graduated from high school. It took me a while to decide to continue my education, but I knew right away what I wanted to study. It was difficult to get accepted into the nursing program, but Suzie helped me prepare, and I made it."

"Congratulations," he said without any hint of insincerity. He meant the word, and his direct gaze told her as much. In fact, it was too direct. She looked away.

"How far into the program are you?" he asked, sinking onto the edge of the desk.

"I've got about six months left before I start my clinicals. I'm really looking forward to that. I know it sounds strange, because I'm shy in crowds and other situations, but one-on-one with a patient? Helping a doctor? That's a venue I can manage."

"Impressive," he said. "Sounds like it's where you thrive. One-on-one."

"I do," she admitted, still feeling his direct gaze without allowing herself to meet it. "I've always done better with the individual rather than the crowd."

"I like that," Maddox said. "A lot of times, that's how many problems are solved. Working with individuals. My line of work isn't much different."

Adelie almost laughed at this. His line of work was totally different.

"You appeal to crowds," she argued.

He rested his hands on the desk's edge on either side of him. "I do, but if the individuals in those crowds aren't enjoying themselves, then I haven't done my job. Everything in Wonderland was designed to appeal to the individual's experience. And considering that expression about how no two people have ever read the same book..."

"Edmund Wilson," Adelie said. "Nice." She'd heard the adage before. People were so different, even reading the same words, their experience in a story would vary based on their own personal experiences and tastes. It meant her experience reading *Alice's Adventures in Wonderland* would never be the same as anyone else's, because there was no one else like her.

"The individual," Maddox said pointedly with a smile.

Her unease lifted just enough.

Silence basked in the sunlight between them. Adelie chewed her lip, trying to think of something to say, a new topic they could pass back and forth that would keep him here.

"I've been having a thought," Maddox said, saving her the trouble.

"Oh yeah? What's that?"

He rested his weight on the desk and crossed his ankles on the carpet. "How would you feel about a honeymoon?"

Okay, not what she'd expected him to say. "A honeymoon?"

"Sure, why not?" he said. "We could get out of Vermont. Go somewhere exotic, where you won't have to worry about being recognized. At least for a few days. We could get to know one another better. What do you think?"

Adelie waited for the joke to follow, but Maddox's gaze was focused and serious, and if she didn't know any better, hopeful. He *wanted* her to say yes.

She scooted to the edge of the bed. "Where would we go?"

"Wherever you want."

"You mean—?"

Inhaling, Maddox rose, crossed the room, and settled onto the edge of the bed beside her. Adelie's insides went into instant alert. She couldn't think with him this close to her, not when they were talking about something like this.

Either Maddox was unaffected, or he handled their proximity better than she did.

"Where have you always dreamed of going?"

Adelie didn't have to think. "Paris. I've always wanted to go to France."

His brow lifted. "You got it," he said. "Paris, it is."

"Just like that? You can snap your fingers and we'll head out?" She had schoolwork to keep up with, but they had computers and internet in Europe, didn't they? How long were they going to be gone?

"Do you have a passport?" Maddox asked.

"I—I do," she said. "Suzie got one for a school trip and talked me into getting mine at the same time." Though she had yet to stamp anything into it.

"And your classes?" he asked. "Do you need to attend anything in person?"

She swallowed, attempting to rein in the giddiness sweltering in her chest. "It's all online. I'll be able to manage."

Maddox's smile shot heat through her. He pulled his phone from his pocket and began typing. "I'll have Duncan's assistant set everything up. She helps me out sometimes when stuff like this comes up."

Adelie grew fidgety. She glanced at her suitcase, still trying to come to grips with the fact that Maddox could call someone else's assistant to help him. Why didn't he have one of his own? Maybe he and Duncan were better friends than she'd originally thought.

"Good thing I haven't unpacked yet," she said.

Maddox rested his hands on his thighs. "You'll be all set. Although, I hope you know you can make this space yours. I want you to be comfortable here."

Adelie cleared her throat and stood. She wasn't sure how to explain her feelings to him. With time, she was sure he might be right. She could be settled here, but she wasn't to that point yet. And until she was, her clothes would remain in the suitcase.

He was preoccupied with his phone for several more moments before lowering it again.

"Looks like we can leave tomorrow. How does that sound?

She exhaled through a small part in her lips. Tomorrow.

"Sounds unbelievable," she said.

Maddox stood, lingering near her for several more ticks of the clock. "Okay, then."

She clasped her hands in front of her. "Okay."

It was all she could do to remain standing until he turned and strolled from the room. The moment he closed the door behind him, her knees buckled. She crumpled onto the bed behind her. How could this be happening? She was married to a billionaire, and now he was taking her on a honeymoon. To Paris.

It wasn't only the total recognizability of the Eiffel Tower, or the fact that the city was some sort of central hub for fashion, food, music, and art. It was the romance of the place, the architecture, the language she loved and had tried learning more than once but always ended up forgetting because she had no one around to speak it with.

Paris. The corner cafes she'd yearned to sit at, the bridges, the token walk down the Champs Elysée.

Adelie wasn't entirely sure what to expect, but then again, her entire relationship with Maddox had been that way. Unpredictable twists and turns at every corner. Not to mention theirs was a marriage in name only. He hadn't even kissed her for goodness' sake. This wasn't going to be a honeymoon the way others celebrated them.

Still, he'd said he wanted to get to know her. Would a kiss be part of that?

18

Maddox tapped his hands on his knees in a quiet rhythm, uncertain of what to say. Adelie sat on the backseat across from him as Kirk neared his private airfield, but she hadn't uttered a single word to him since they'd left home.

She'd been so reticent about this entire trip, from the minute he presented it to her yesterday. Did she really want this, or was she just going along because he'd suggested it?

He got the feeling this was typical of her. To sacrifice her own needs in order to please others. What could he do to help her relax around him? To show him who she really was?

They'd had a moment on the carousel when he'd felt as though her guard was down, and then again, after the incident at Coleman's. She'd bared herself to him as she demanded he take every sign featuring her down. She'd been assertive then. Self-assured. Why didn't she allow herself to be that way all the time? What happened in her past to make her so timid, so afraid of people?

More than anything, Maddox wanted Adelie to feel secure around him, to open up to him. To be his friend in addition to his sudden wife. Considering the way those men had treated her at Coleman's, this was the whole reason Maddox hadn't kissed her at their wedding. He was nothing like those losers. He wanted to make it clear he would push nothing on her.

Kirk turned into the airport and pulled up next to a small plane. Adelie rested a hand on the window the way a child would and scooted forward, as though taken by surprise. This couldn't be her first time seeing an airplane.

"Have you flown before?" he asked.

"Never," she said without looking at him.

"Then this should be a real treat for you." It was too bad, in some ways. If she'd never been in a commercial plane, she couldn't fully appreciate how spacious the jet Duncan's assistant, Rosabel, had chartered would be.

Maddox had considered purchasing his own plane, but he didn't fly all that much, not really. He usually chartered one through a private company, and they'd always been readily available whenever he'd needed it.

The aircraft, with its pointed nose, sleek, thin wings, and angled tail that had always reminded Maddox of a dorsal fin, remained ready with its side door hanging down and serving as a staircase for their entrance.

"Is this yours?"

Her awe over what seemed to him to be simple things put everything in a new light. He'd flown in a jet like this so many times he couldn't count, but with her, this seemed like the first time. Had the plane always been this small? Had he ever paid this much attention to its smooth design and tiny windows?

"No, I prefer to charter one when I need it," he said. "Are you ready?"

"To see Paris? I've always been ready."

She exited the car, and Maddox slid out behind her, chuckling at her guileless pronouncement and enjoying the opportunity to stretch. That was one thing about using a smaller jet for a long flight like this. Compared to a commercial flight's cramped seats, this jet had only a handful, leaving space to roam around. They would have more room to spread out as the hours dragged on.

The pilot strolled toward the plane, wearing the uniform that bespoke his profession and added a touch of class to his posture. Maddox shook his hand.

"Hey, there, Anthony," he greeted.

"Maddox." His brows lifted as Adelie approached and joined Maddox's side. "Looks like you've got some company this time."

"I do. This is my wife, Adelie."

The most becoming shade of pink touched her cheeks. She offered a hand to Anthony.

"Nice to meet you," she said.

"You as well. I didn't even hear there were wedding bells for you. Congratulations. Paris sounds like a great destination to celebrate."

"It is," Adelie agreed. Behind her, Kirk passed their bags toward a man in a vest who helped load them into a cargo hold beneath the jet.

"Shall we?" Anthony gestured for Adelie to board first. Lowering her chin, she turned and made the small incline up the ladder and into the plane. Maddox followed and nearly stumbled into the back of her, she'd stopped so suddenly.

"Oh, wow," Adelie said with a hand to her chest. The luxurious cabin was spacious, offering two plush, leather chairs beside a leather couch that covered the length of the jet's right-hand side.

"Like it?" Maddox said softly into her ear. He took satisfaction in the goosebumps rising on the skin at her neck.

She turned toward him, close enough for the skin of her cheek to brush his. Startling, she stepped forward. A flush of color climbed into her cheeks again, and she tucked her hair behind her ear and hugged one arm to her side as she looked everywhere but at him.

"It's amazing. It feels more like a hotel room or something than an airplane."

"I think you'll really like that," Maddox said, sizzling at her response to him. If he had only one goal from now on, it would be to make her blush like that again. "It's nice to travel in something that gives you a little breathing room."

"Can I—can I sit down?"

Maddox laughed. "Sure, you can. You think I'd make you stand the entire time? Besides, I think we need to be buckled in for takeoff."

Adelie didn't notice him teasing her. Instead, she settled onto the cream leather seat facing the front of the plane. Maddox sank into the one across from her. She immediately buckled her seatbelt and then sat rigidly, again as though unsure how to behave.

Was she nervous about the flight? Many people got airsick or claustrophobic on planes. Maddox tried to think of something that might put her at ease.

"I like to leave this time of the day," he said. "You know, mid-afternoon. That way we fly all night and get some sleep, and then it's almost evening when we get to France. Easier to deal with jet lag that way."

"I never would have thought of that," Adelie said, her shoulders relaxing just enough. "I'll have to tell my cousin Ella."

"Oh? Is she going to Paris as well?"

Adelie lifted a shoulder. "I'm not sure about Paris, but she will be heading for her own honeymoon soon."

"What a coincidence." He wondered if she'd chosen Paris because she really wanted to go there or because she hadn't been able to think of anything else.

Maddox crossed an ankle onto the opposite knee. "Are you close with your cousin?"

Again, Adelie's posture relaxed enough to be visible. "We were close as children," she said. "We lost touch until a few Christmases ago when she had a bit of a crisis. Her stepmom framed her for stealing office supplies from the company she worked for."

"You're kidding."

"Nope," Adelie said. "Just before the whole fallout, she'd also been uninvited for Christmas by the same stepmom, and so our grandma—Grammy Larsen, not Grandma Carroll—got Suzie and me to come help clean Ella's apartment and make her Christmas lunch."

"Sounds like you made her holiday."

Adelie smiled at the memory, and Maddox wished he could read her thoughts.

"Yeah, I think we did. But Ella always did so much for everyone else, she deserved it. Anyway, she's getting married to the guy who accused her of stealing."

Not what he was expecting. Maddox burst out with laughter. "Now that's a story."

The flight passed as he expected, and yet not at all. He and Adelie spent much of the first several hours rapt in one another's conversation. They talked about his mom, and then the conversation shifted to her parents.

"You talk about your grandparents a lot," Maddox said. "What about your mom and dad?"

Adelie closed in. He was starting to notice the way her eyes shifted, the way she tucked her chin to her chest, whenever there was a topic that made her uncomfortable.

"They weren't around much," she hedged. "They...passed away."

"How did they die?" he asked.

"Car accident." Her reply was blunt. She didn't elaborate. He suspected there was more to it, but that she wasn't ready to divulge anything else.

His chest ached for the pain in her posture. She confessed her parents had left her and Suzie when they'd both been small, but also the deep love she felt for her grandparents who'd raised her when her parents failed to. They talked about Adelie's dreams once she was done with nursing school.

Night soon fell, and Maddox retrieved blankets for himself and Adelie, who was eyeing the couch with deprivation in her sleepy eyes.

"Please," he said, helping her settle in. She rolled her back to him and was fast asleep within minutes.

It took him a little longer to drift off. Though his chair did recline, and he was quite relaxed, he watched her, grateful he'd decided on this. They needed a trip like this together. Something to help ease her mind—and his—after their rushed wedding and the occurrence at the grocery store.

The plane's gentle hum was like a lullaby. Before he knew it, Maddox blinked sleep from his eyes and took in the jet's dimmed cabin. Adelie was crouched near the window, peering out at the incoming destination. He rubbed his eyes and stared at his watch. Had he really slept that long?

The pilot's voice came over the intercom. "Good evening, Mr. and Mrs. Hatter. We'll soon be arriving at the Charles de Gaulle International Airport. If you look out to your right, you'll see the famous Eiffel Tower greeting us as we close in."

Adelie released a small squeak. She dashed to the plane's opposite side. "Oh goodness, there it is," she said breathily.

Maddox set his blanket aside and joined her.

"So it is," he said in response to the structure's needlelike shape spearing into the sky. It wasn't yet dark enough for them to light the structure, but he found he couldn't wait to see what Adelie's reaction to the Eiffel Tower's sparkle would be.

"Maddox."

His name, spoken so tenderly on her lips, gave him pause.

Slowly, she shifted her gaze to him. "You have no idea what this means to me."

A small tingle pinged in his chest. "We're not even there yet," he said with a chuckle.

"How can you say that when the Eiffel Tower is *right there* in front of you?" She brought her attention back to the window.

Maddox fought the desire to lead her away from the window and into his arms. What was this pull she had over him?

~

Anthony landed the plane with precision, and soon they were disembarking, retrieving their bags from the accommodating staff, going through customs and security, and finally entering the awaiting car. Adelie's attention was stolen with every passing sight. Even the streets and countryside were incredible to her.

In her mind's eye, she saw Alice peering into her rabbit hole. Curiosity had gotten the better of her; she'd tumbled in, and now Adelie could sympathize more than ever. This was *Paris*. Her own personal rabbit hole, where she felt as if she were falling slowly and still unable to grasp every new thing around her.

The car pulled to a stop before an elegant building curved to fit the corner it sat on. Its rooftop was of the typical Parisian style, with its dark roof contrasting the cream-colored brick and featuring a series of awnings. Each subsequent window along the brick was joined with an iron railing similar to what was found at Wonderland.

Adelie stood as though her feet were on a lazy Susan. She kept turning and rotating, taking in every sight she possibly could as though this would be the last time she had her vision. She took in the hotel's name on the gold plate beside the door, as well as on a banner projecting from the building's side, as the driver placed their bags on the sidewalk beside her and Maddox.

Maddox offered the driver a tip and a *"Merci beaucoup,"* before turning back to her.

"We're staying at an Elir hotel?"

"Should we have stayed somewhere else?" Maddox picked up their suitcases and led the way inside.

Light was everywhere she looked. The furniture of the lobby was rounded and elegant, the windows speckled every few feet and offered a view of the street, and lamps dotted the space between each of them as well. Several people stood near the decorative glass tiles that separated the seating area from the check-in desk.

"You act like you've never seen a hotel before," Maddox whispered to her in the same low tone he'd used when she'd been stopped short at first sight of his jet's insides. It had the same effect on her now as it had then, drawing shivers down her spine.

"I haven't," Adelie admitted. "At least not one like this." The only time she'd stayed in a hotel had been at the Motel 6 in Harrisburg, Pennsylvania, when her parents still had custody of her and Suzie, before her mom had left and before they'd been taken from their father. And that was nothing compared to this.

"The Elir Paris," Maddox said. "It is something."

"*You* act like you come here all the time," Adelie said, walking with him toward the check-in desk.

"I've been here a few times. Once during college, to attend a friend's wedding. And once with...well, it doesn't matter."

"With whom?"

"Just some friends," he said distractedly, pulling out his wallet to show his ID to the woman behind the desk.

Her stomach fisted. Was he keeping something from her? Why not just tell her who he'd been with? She supposed she had parts of her past she'd rather forget—mostly regarding her parents. Maybe it was one of those instances.

The woman at the desk handed Maddox a key, and he bid her, "*Merci,*" before turning to Adelie.

"Sounds like our room is ready. Come on."

"*Our*—room?" She scurried to keep pace. After a brief elevator ride, the busboy led the way down a decadent hallway, pausing to open door 401 for them.

Adelie lingered in the hallway, not only distracted by the way he inserted the room key into a nook on the wall to have it power the lights in the room, but by the fact that he brought both her and Maddox's suitcase into the same space.

"Have a good evening," he said in a decidedly French accent that kinked inside her stomach, before tipping his hat and leaving her alone with her husband.

Several ticks passed as realization dawned. He hadn't guided her to a separate room because there wasn't one. Maddox had booked only one room for them. For their *honeymoon.* The thought heightened every one of her senses and she suddenly felt too warm.

They were married. They should share a room, right?

Tucking his wallet into his back jeans pocket, he turned. With the door closed behind her, and the open living area behind him, the space between them shrunk. Maddox seemed to catch on to her surprise as evidenced by the slight jump in the muscle of his jaw.

"I hope this is okay." He gestured to the ornate but comfortable room. "Duncan's assistant didn't know our marriage was anything but impulsive ecstasy, so she booked a single room. I can get another one if you'd like."

Adelie's throat closed. Sharing a room with Maddox. It wouldn't be what others thought it was, and not only that, but she wasn't sure she wanted to be apart from him in a foreign city. Closer brought more comfort. At least, that was what she told herself.

"No, this is fine."

"The suite setup here is great. We can each have our own area. I'll just camp out on the pullout couch." He gestured to the ornament behind him, bedecked with silver pillows. "You can have the bedroom."

"No—I can take the couch."

Bemused, Maddox crossed the few steps toward her and touched a finger to her elbow. "Mrs. Hatter, take the bedroom. It's okay."

Adelie attempted to wet her lips. He'd never called her that before.

"Are you tired? Maybe we can grab some dinner, though I do have to warn you, it won't be quick. The French don't do fast food the way we do in America. At least not where I prefer to eat. They like their courses, and if you know what's good for you, you'll enjoy every bite."

She was too exhilarated to feel tired. She'd flown on a jet and was in France. France! This was a dream come true. Now to eat their food? She'd never had French cuisine.

"Sure, I'd love to grab some dinner."

"Perfect. I'll make sure the restaurant is open."

Adelie took a minute to freshen up, changed her clothes, and met Maddox outside the bathroom door.

"I'm just finishing up," he said, bending to rinse his mouth after brushing his teeth.

She peered around, taking in the light switches and electric plugs. It didn't seem that much different from home and yet was completely new, from their placement on the wall to their shapes.

"Come on in," he said.

Feeling strange about sharing a sink with him, she shuffled in, hoping to skirt past him before he finished. Mid-stride, Maddox turned for his towel hanging on the rack near the mirror and brushed against her.

"Cramped quarters," he said.

"I don't mind." Momentarily mesmerized by the field of green in his eyes, she hurried to clarify. "I had to share a bathroom with Suzie until we got the plumbing fixed."

Though something told her this was going to be a lot different than sharing with her sister.

Smirking, and keeping his eyes on hers, Maddox reached for the towel once more. The smell of his cologne wafted to her. Her entire body stiffened. This was the closest to him she'd ever been. Even at their wedding there had been a good two feet between them. And though he'd stood beside her as she'd ridden the peacock on the carousel, they'd been out in the open air. This was a confined pocket of the universe, a place where neither of them seemed all that eager to move from.

Adelie managed to find her voice. "This has happened more and more since I met you."

"What has?"

"The feeling that I've changed size," she said. "When you look at me that way, I feel like—"

He lowered the towel. "What do you feel?"

Words dangled from the tip of her tongue. She wanted to tell him he gave her courage, he made her bold and adventurous, and she envisioned herself as the kind of woman she'd always wanted to be, the one who wasn't afraid to take risks, to put herself out there, to speak to someone new or assert herself the way she knew she'd like to.

As a nurse, bedside manner was important. She knew she needed to have a little more confidence and be able to talk to complete strangers. Inwardly, she hadn't changed from the shy dormouse she'd always been, but with him, she felt like she could be more

For some reason, she couldn't bring herself to admit as much.

She dipped her head and backed into the sink, clutching her toothbrush in her hand. "Just excited."

Maddox cleared his throat and backed away too, which gave her enough distance to rotate and brush her teeth and ruminate over all the things she wished she'd said.

They took a cab to a restaurant whose name Adelie attempted to pronounce and missed. Her high school and college French seemed to be doing her little good now that she was here. She did, however, attempt to redeem herself by reading items on the menu, to which the waiter gave her congratulatory nods every few seconds.

Maddox wasn't kidding about the dinner's complexity. The meal was a series of courses, from soup to a salad, to the haricots verts alongside coq au vin, and then a decadent cheese course before finishing off with the dessert. Adelie had to say, the cheese was her favorite.

Though she'd slept on the flight, the tiredness of traveling halfway across the world began catching up with her. Her eyelids threatened to droop.

"Ready to crash?" Maddox asked, wiping his mouth and placing his napkin on the table.

Adelie shook herself enough to give him an acquiescent nod. "That would probably be a good idea."

With dark rims beneath his eyes, he appeared as tired as she felt. She had some chagrin over that. She'd taken the couch—on his insistence, but still, she'd taken it. Had he been able to sleep at all during their flight?

Once they returned to the Elir, their conversation crashed to a halt. She barely bade him goodnight before tumbling gratefully into bed. She was too tired to even consider that an extremely handsome man—her husband—was sleeping just a wall away.

19

T he sound struck the sides of her subconscious. It came multiple times in a row, tap, tap, tapping straight into her fuzzy dreams. Dreams of flying, of sharing the jet's leather couch with Maddox and feeling his arm secure her to his side, teaching her the definition of spooning...

Tap. Tap. Tap.

His nose was nearing her earlobe. Her imaginary Maddox's warm breath teased the hair on her neck. She rotated to face him, placing her in a completely inappropriate position if they were anything but married.

But they were married...

Tap. Tap. "Adelie?"

She blinked away the last dregs of the dream. Her hand spread to the silky sheets beside her, only to find the bed empty.

"You awake?"

"Yeah," she muttered, pulling the blanket to her shoulders and attempting to ram away the budding emotions brought on from the dream. What was that about? She'd never cuddled with a man like that before. Why should she fantasize about it with *him*? "Come on in."

The knob turned, and Maddox entered, but he came bearing gifts. In his hand was a silver tray hosting two silver domes, a pair of small glasses, and a carafe of what looked like milk.

"Good morning," he said, moving deeper into the room. He looked husky and masculine in a Wonderland t-shirt. Washed gray, it bore the park's logo and the phrase, *We're all mad here.*

"Sorry to wake you, but I realized I didn't tell you what was on the schedule for today."

"We have a schedule?" Adelie sat up in her blankets, propped the pillow behind her, and nestled against it. She reached for her phone—which she hadn't been able to charge last night, thanks to her lack of a plug that fit these different outlets—eager to check the time. Wow, ten-thirty? She wondered what time it was back home in Vermont.

Maddox roosted on the edge of the bed, tray still in his hands.

"We do. Wanna talk about it over breakfast?"

A smile took over her face. "I can't believe you brought me breakfast in bed. And that you let me sleep in so long."

"I thought you might appreciate the extra rest."

"That smells delicious," she said, smoothing out the blankets between them so he could place the tray on a semi-flat surface. Maddox lowered it, adjusting the tray so one domed plate faced Adelie and the other lay before him.

Together, the two of them dug into their plates.

"Bread?" Adelie said, taking her small servings and enjoying the side of fruit.

"The French love their breads. You should try some of this jam."

Adelie relished the taste of the freshly baked croissant and the strawberry jam, washing it down with a glass of water. "So, you said we have a schedule today?"

Maddox took a drink of his milk as well. "I'd like to take you on a tour of the city."

Adelie lowered her glass and gaped at him. "Really?"

"Really."

"Maddox, I'd love that."

"I'm glad to hear it." He held her gaze for several moments before she glanced away.

He cleared his throat. "Well. I'll let you get dressed. Our bus tour leaves in about an hour, is that enough time?"

"Bus tour?" Her excitement over sharing the city with Maddox alone waned.

"Sure." He waited for her to place her napkin down before retrieving the tray. "It's the best way to see all the tourist sights, you know, the really popular ones most people come here to see. I did it once before, it's pretty amazing. We can go at our own pace, pick which sites we want to stop at, the works."

"Sounds good," she said. "Maddox?" She caught him before he reached the door. He paused and peered back. "Thank you for breakfast. It was a stunning way to start the day."

His mouth twisted against a smile. "Be prepared for it to get even better." He winked before traipsing out and closing the door behind him.

Giddy in a way she hadn't been in years, Adelie dressed with a bounce in every step. She couldn't grasp how ridiculously excited she was to see the city she'd fantasized over since she took her first French class her freshman year of high school. That had been over ten years ago, and yet the intrigue and attraction of Paris, of everything French, had never lost its appeal. If anything, it had only increased.

"And here I am," she said to herself as she checked her floral blouse and jeans in the mirror. The day promised to be sunny but cold, so she added a blue sweater to the ensemble and strolled out.

Maddox's brow lifted with appreciation. His light green eyes, so much like colored glass, flicked from her shoulders to her toes and back to her face.

"You ready?" he asked.

"Yep." She slung her purse on her shoulder and joined him in getting to the street below.

They toured the city on a double-decker bus splashed with stripes of orange, purple, and white. Adelie was grateful Maddox led the way to the upper level, and while it took more time during the hop-on, hop-off segments of the city, she was able to see more of it during the interim from an upper vantage point.

Every twist, every turn, stole her breath. She gobbled up views of the buildings, the Louvre's token glass pyramid, the Paris Opera House, and the sad remains of Notre Dame—or what was left of it after the fire that demolished the beautiful structure a few years before.

The bus stopped at all the important places. The Louvre, the Eiffel Tour, the Champs Elysée, which let out at the L'Arc de Triomphe. The architecture was spectacular; it was all completely surreal.

While returning to the tour bus stop after strolling past shops from which she could never hope to purchase anything, Maddox's phone buzzed. He'd answered calls from Duncan, from investors and handled other business on occasion, but after a fleeting glance at the screen, he returned the phone to his pocket.

"Not going to answer?" Adelie asked.

He sniffed, allowing his hand to grasp hers. Adelie's stomach burned at the contact. He'd never held her hand like this in public before. Like they were a couple.

"Is this okay?" he asked.

She didn't need him to clarify what he was asking. She squeezed his fingers in hers. "Yes," she said quietly.

Adelie noticed Maddox's phone buzz several more times along their journey from the street and back to their tour bus. Each time, he glanced at the screen, only to pocket the phone once more without replying.

Who could be calling him? And why would he ignore it?

They stopped for lunch at a small corner café where the pastries were the flakiest, creamiest she'd ever tasted. She was starting to see the appeal of eating so much bread, though she topped it off with a refreshing café crème that battled the chill in her fingertips. Maddox rested his phone on the table, and a name blared on the screen once more.

"Who's Ruby?" Adelie asked, unable to help her glimpse of the name and the picture of a beautiful woman with dark hair, plump lips, and black eyeliner flaring into delicate little wings that accentuated her stunning eyes.

"Hmm?"

She gestured to his phone with her fork. "Ruby. Is she the one who keeps calling you? Who is she?"

He covered the phone with his palm and slid it to his lap as though it was a card that had just been dealt to him. "She's no one," he said. "An old friend."

Adelie's eyes narrowed. "The same 'old friend' you went to Paris with before?"

Like a knee-jerk reaction, Maddox shifted his attention away from her. Adelie's forehead knitted at the invisible barrier forming between them and at his lack of response—which was basically an affirmation. Whoever this Ruby was, she'd meant something to him at one point in time. Whether she did now or not, Adelie couldn't be sure.

Her jaw clenched. He was acting so distracted, so different from the warmth he'd displayed during breakfast and again throughout the tour. Did he regret being here with her? Did he wish he was with whoever this Ruby was? Why didn't he just answer the call?

Doubt sifted through the happy emotions she'd been basking in since they'd arrived. Scenario after scenario sifted through her mind, of who Ruby could be. He wouldn't have offered to marry Adelie if he'd been in a relationship with someone else, she told herself. But the internal argument wasn't convincing enough to soothe her worries.

Maddox gripped his phone and rose from the small, circular table. "We should hurry so we don't miss our next stop."

Adelie didn't move right away. Confusion was still a crease in her forehead. Their tour was something they could take at their own pace. It wasn't as though the bus was sitting at the stop waiting for them. Even if they missed one, another would be along shortly after.

Conflict swarmed inside of her. She wanted Maddox to know how grateful she was for his help after the Coleman's incident. She wanted him to know how incredible this moment was—or how incredible it would have been sans the mysterious phone call. He'd put his life on hold to marry her. To take her on a fake honeymoon. That had to mean something.

For Adelie, courage had never come easily. This was her Wonderland, to explore a completely foreign world with him. Part of her wanted to admit it wouldn't matter whether they were in France or back in Vermont, she wanted to let him know she was ready for the journey. To let him know whatever he was hiding from her didn't matter.

But *something* still stood in the way, she thought as she stared out at the still water of the Seine and one of Paris's many bridges intersecting through the city. Pedestrians strolled aimlessly along its wooden planks. And that *something* buzzed in his pocket again.

Maddox pulled out the phone, turning his back to Adelie.

She let her fingers linger on the table's edge until she managed to collect her wits and make her way to him. He couldn't keep denying it. The least she could do was point it out to him.

"You've been ignoring her calls all day," Adelie said.

Maddox angled his head away and had the gall to appear startled. As though he hadn't heard his phone vibrating throughout their tour.

He crinkled his nose. "How do you know that was a her?"

"I have eyes." Adelie smiled in an attempt to cover the uneasy speculation swimming inside of her. He'd mentioned coming to Paris with someone else before. Was it with whoever this Ruby was?

"Are you going to tell me who she is? You don't have to. I mean, I know this is just a favor you're doing me, and we're not on a real honeymoon or anything like that. I don't want to keep you from anything."

What was she doing, saying something like that? The words hurt on their way out. She didn't realize how heartless it sounded until they'd already escaped. The truth was, she was falling for him. An admission like this made it sound like he was as disposable to her as she felt to him in that moment.

Maddox's green eyes glinted with realization. A crease appeared between his brows, and he scowled at his phone.

"You're right," he said, resting a hand on Adelie's arm. He then brandished the phone. "Hang on, I'll be right back."

With determination, he strolled away from her, away from the wooden pedestrian bridge they'd paused near and its view of the Seine running right through the city. The river appeared almost concrete, like another street.

Adelie waited a moment near the bridge's side, taking in its lampposts and the benches lining every handful of feet. She remembered hearing a story of a love lock bridge in Paris, where tourists would attach a padlock to its barrier and throw the key into the Seine as a symbol of their undying love. It hadn't been all that long ago that the number of locks attached to the bridges began compromising the bridge's safety and stability because of their massive weight, and the mayor of Paris had ordered the locks to be removed.

Had this bridge been a love lock bridge?

Whether it had been or not, this was Paris, the City of Lights, arguably one of the most romantic places in the world. It wasn't exactly the ideal location to get ditched.

Adelie couldn't deny that was how she felt watching Maddox turn away from her to answer the call of an extremely beautiful woman who he refused to tell her anything about.

The same jealousy that had gnawed at her during their lunch turned from a drip to a deluge. She wasn't unfamiliar with the sensation. She'd spent the entirety of her teenage and adult life watching every guy she'd ever been interested in show interest in someone else.

She hadn't had a claim on any of them, though, so the heartache that usually accompanied those instances had been relatively easy to manage.

This, though. Like it or not, she did have a claim on Maddox. A huge claim. Adelie tried to argue it away, to tell herself she shouldn't be so rash, that regardless of the M-word joining them, their relationship wasn't that serious and never would be. While she'd wished their wedding was more of the romantic variety, she hadn't realized until that moment how badly she wished their relationship was everything that word stood for and more.

An unforeseen wave of sadness swept over her as she watched his back, as he continued his conversation, as he made his way farther and farther from her.

Before he'd taken the call, he'd said she was right. He'd told her to wait for him.

She was right? Right about what, how he shouldn't let her keep him from talking to whoever this other woman was?

Adelie stepped out of herself for a moment. What was she doing here? She was in this heritage-rich city, standing on a bridge, surrounded by dozens of others but feeling utterly alone. Adelie hadn't known herself since she met Maddox. He was constantly trying to get her to be something she wasn't. A model. A wife.

She should have stood her ground from the start. Then again, was there a better time to start doing just that?

The old Adelie would have waited near the bridge. She would have hung around while her husband was off chatting on the phone with another woman, too scared to navigate her way back to their hotel room on her own.

She was done being that timid dormouse. She was ready to be the Cheshire Cat, living each day with a smile, coming and going as she pleased. If that meant she was a little mad, she'd take it.

Not waiting to catch his attention, or seeing if he would make his way back toward her, Adelie walked away from the fence and down the bridge. She had money. She could find her own hotel room. Maybe in America, back where everyone knew her as the Alice to his Wonderland, she had to play the part to the role she'd agreed to. But here in France?

She was ready to be the woman she'd always dreamed of being. Larger than life, confident, secure, no longer letting anyone else dictate her actions or make her live in fear. She was also beyond eager to have her own room to manage her own heartbreak without having a witness.

20

A delie made her way to the nearest bus stop and boarded, feeling strangely out of focus. She sat on the first available seat, not bothering to make her way to the bus's upper level the way she'd done with Maddox, and she rode her way through the city toward the Elir.

The longer Adelie rode, the more she began to awaken from her selfishness. What was she thinking? Maddox had invited her here. He'd paid for their airfare, the hotel, he'd arranged everything. He'd been so kind to her. She was being petty over a silly phone call. It didn't mean anything, and if it did, the least she could do was allow him to explain who it was.

She checked her phone, eager to text him and apologize, only to press the button multiple times and receive no response.

"Great," she muttered to herself. She'd forgotten its low battery during the rush of the day, the tour, the sights. Not having a correct plug to fit the European electrical outlets, she hadn't been able to charge it the night before. And with Maddox's romantic breakfast and the exhilaration of the day, she hadn't thought to check with him before they left.

Now not only was she completely alone, but she had no phone to boot.

The Elir's grandiose, brick form made her heart leap. Adelie took the next stop and got off, scuttling her way along the street, inside the hotel—stopping in the gift shop to purchase a European phone charger—and up to their room. At least she still had her key.

She hoped Maddox might be there waiting for her, but the room was quiet and empty. Carved and hollow as well, Adelie shuffled in, inserted her key into the hub above the light switches to activate the room's electricity and lights, and closed the door behind her.

"How did it get like this?" she asked the quiet.

Behind her, the key sounded, and the door flung open. It would have knocked into her if she hadn't taken several astonished steps away.

Maddox appeared in the doorway, a look of desperation on his handsome face.

"Adelie?" His voice sounded so frantic. So afraid.

Guilt wrenched her as cold, stark relief washed over him at the sight of her. "Maddox!"

In a moment, she was in his arms. "Oh my gosh," he said, bending his nose to her shoulder. "I thought you got kidnapped. I thought something had happened to you. Why didn't you answer my calls and texts?"

He pulled her away, holding her at arms' length to get a better look at her face. "I considered searching the city, but decided to head back here right away, just in case."

"I—I'm so sorry," she said, touched by his alarm and intensity. This wasn't the reaction of a man who didn't care about her. The realization only made her regret worse for taking off the way she did. "My phone died on the way back to the hotel."

He stared at her as though he'd never seen her before. "Why

did you leave like that? I asked you to wait for me, I thought you'd be there, but I turned around and you were gone. I've been hunting all over the place trying to find you."

Adelie ducked her head. She was such an idiot. All over jealousy, over stupid, trivial jealousy and pride. She'd never battled with pride before now. Why did it have to go rearing its head? She didn't even know who Ruby was. Why did she have to go and jump to conclusions about her?

Still, they were on a honeymoon. A weird, platonic type of honeymoon, but Maddox had said he wanted them to get to know one another. How could they when he was clearly keeping this other woman a secret from her?

Then again, it never occurred to her that she didn't know the name of Duncan's assistant. She thought Maddox had mentioned it, but was it Ruby? If so, why didn't he just tell Adelie as much, or answer the calls?

"I'm sorry. I guess..."

"Why didn't you wait for me?" he said again.

"Why should I?" Her voice was deadly soft. "Why did you marry me at all when you're clearly in another relationship? Who is Ruby?"

Maddox groaned and rubbed a hand over his face. He ambled past her toward his couch instead of answering.

Adelie trudged to her own bed in the next room. She and Suzie had gotten in plenty of fights, but this was so different. Suzie was her sister. She knew her sarcastic habits and personal tendencies to defend with throwing things back at Adelie.

Adelie had never gotten into a disagreement with someone who wasn't family before. Not serious, not like this. Why did it matter who Ruby was? Why couldn't she just let it go?

Saying vows to Maddox in the Westville City Hall made it matter. She didn't realize how seriously she'd taken this marriage until now. She wanted this to be a real honeymoon.

But it wasn't. This wasn't a real marriage, where people wedded out of love for the other and a deep, serious commitment to honor the other person in sickness and in health, in both answered and ignored phone calls. This was another brand, another billboard, a way for Maddox to assuage his guilt for having put Adelie in an uncomfortable situation.

So, she'd gone and married him on a whim. Good grief. She needed some serious therapy.

This was the photo shoot all over again. Yet again, she'd made the mistake of settling. Of jumping into something she didn't really want. This wasn't how a honeymoon was supposed to be. He was supposed to adore her, not be constantly interrupted by another woman.

More than that, he was supposed to have already loved her enough to present her with a lock, ready to throw away the key that would open his heart to anyone else but her.

It wasn't real, and it never had been.

The thought panged inside of her, the way it had been doing all day. They couldn't force this, no matter how hard they tried to make it look like they had. Suddenly, she wanted to go home. Why did Vermont have to be an ocean away?

Maddox was sitting on the couch he had yet to pull out. Hunched over so his elbows rested on his knees, he held his head in his hands and stared at the floor.

"Are you okay?" Adelie asked, approaching. She'd jumped to conclusions. She'd made assumptions instead of being open from the start. Worst of all, she'd mistreated him, worse than she'd even realized. He'd been scared, worried for her safety. She should never have done that to him.

"I'm so sorry, Maddox."

Maddox sat up. His eyes were sad, and frustration furrowed his brow. Regardless, he offered her a hand. "Will you sit with me?"

Adelie took it, allowing him to lead her to take the empty cushion beside him. She expected him to release her hand, but instead, he held it, stroking her skin with his thumb. The sensation served to relax her shoulders, and she settled near his side, craving the closeness and its reminder that, despite her mistake, he hadn't yet written her off.

"When I first started Wonderland, I needed some backing. I stumbled across a woman who was confident she could help my little theme park take off. She showered me with praise and carried out every promise she'd made. Soon enough, we found out we had more than a business interest in one another.

"Ruby and I started dating, and our relationship was really great for a while. But she was constantly talking about money, about investments, about all the things we could do by expanding and building new theme parks across the U.S.

"I didn't want that. I'd built Wonderland for my mother, and one park was enough for me. I'd also made plenty of money—I didn't need to go seeking for more. But I thought I was in love with her, and I wanted to support her dreams as well as my own.

"Ruby started pooling money into other places, claiming it would be best for the park. But a lot of the risks she took ended up falling out from underneath me. It caused a strain in our relationship and not only that, with my attention so focused elsewhere, Wonderland's appeal started to plummet too. Profits weren't what they were. Ruby had access to all my accounts and saw everything. And before I knew it, she ended our engagement."

Adelie stroked his forearm, fumbling for words. Her initial reaction was to sympathize with his heartache, but she wasn't exactly sorry Ruby had ended things with him.

"Do you still love her?" she asked.

"No," he said without hesitating.

For some reason, she couldn't allow herself to believe him.

She didn't suppose anyone stopped loving someone else. Not really. Not when you felt enough for another person to want to marry them the right way instead of the rushed, fake way. That made this situation all the worse.

He continued stroking her hand. "I didn't want her to be a part of our trip, Adelie. That's why I was trying to ignore her phone calls. She's been hounding me since she saw the rebrand. I wanted to keep her from finding out about you, but she's relentless and persistent. It's what makes her so successful, I guess. She's not going to give up until I give in and let her meet you."

Adelie was caught short. Her spine straightened. "She wants to meet me? Why?"

"She tends to try and predict success. Sounds like she thinks I'm onto something with you."

Just what kind of success was he talking about here? If it had anything to do with modeling, that had been a one-time thing. She wasn't about to put herself in a similar situation ever again.

Considering Adelie's earlier suspicion, that there had been something more between Maddox and Ruby before Adelie came along, another suspicion filtered in. Adelie had been ripe with jealousy after one stupid phone call featuring Ruby's pretty face on Maddox's screen.

Had the sight of Adelie's face on Maddox's theme park had the same effect on Ruby? Was that why she was doing this?

"She knows I'm your model, but does she—does she know you married me?"

He lowered his head, allowing her hand to slip free from his so he could rake his hands through his hair. "No. I haven't known how to tell her."

"I see."

The answer was enough. They'd been *engaged*. There had

been something between them. If he was hiding Adelie from Ruby, perhaps there was still something between them.

With her hand free, Adelie stood. She couldn't be close to him any longer. She was already growing too attached as it was. He was going to be hard to walk away from, so the sooner she did so, the better.

Maddox's jaw set. "What do you mean?"

"I see," she repeated. "Why you wanted to go to France. To keep me from her."

"Adelie," he said. "I wanted to go to France with you because you're my wife."

The declaration stung the corners of her eyes. She couldn't bring herself to look at him. He said it so tenderly. So straightforward.

"I just…"

"What? You don't believe me?"

"I want to," she said, sniffing. "But—"

"But what?"

Tears blurred her vision. Her throat closed. She hated the way crying affected her. It was such a stupid thing. She couldn't bring herself to say it.

He rose to his feet and cradled her face with his hand. "But what? Tell me. Please."

"I am your wife," she said through her tears. He wiped a stray bead from her cheek. She wished he wouldn't be so attentive right now. Then again, if he wasn't, she wasn't sure she'd be able to say what she needed to. "But it's only a piece of paper."

"How can you say that?" The sorrow in his tone was too raw.

She persisted. "Because it's true. You didn't even kiss me."

Light flickered in his eyes, joined with comprehension. The air between them shifted, thickening and filling with heat.

"Is that what this is about?" he said softly. "You want to be kissed?"

She wanted to retreat. She couldn't, not with the way he held her face in his hands.

"Marriage should be sealed with a kiss." Adelie fought her trembling lower lip.

He tilted in, taking a step and enclosing his arm around her in a single motion. Pressed to his body, her heartbeat ratcheted the way it did when she'd been on one of his roller coasters, trekking up the slow, building climb that would lead to the sudden plunge into speed and exhilaration, to a ride she had no power to stop.

She'd never had the sensation of a man's lips pressed to her own, and this wasn't just any man. This was Maddox Hatter, the man who'd spun her like a top since the moment they'd met.

His lashes brushed his cheeks. His lips hovered inches from hers, and his breath stroked her skin. She waited, aching, craving, wanting. But she couldn't give in.

Adelie closed her eyes. "Don't," she said.

"Don't what?"

"Don't kiss me out of pity or because of what I said. I want you to kiss me because this marriage means something to you." *Because I mean something to you.*

"Adelie." Her name rumbled in his throat. He tightened his hold around her. "It's more than that," he said. "I want it to be more. Please, let me prove it to you."

"No. I'm sorry, Maddox, but I can't do this. Not if you still have feelings for Ruby, not if this is all going to end in heartache. I've never kissed anyone before, but I get the feeling doing so is going to give you too much of me, and I won't be able to recover if I lost that. Good night."

She hurried to her room and shut the door, not wanting him to see her cry.

21

M addox was baffled. He couldn't understand what would make her so hesitant to trust—not only him, but everyone. This was more than shyness, more than uncertainty or hesitation. She'd mentioned how hard it had been when her parents had abandoned her. Was that what made her so resistant to letting people in?

He checked the time back in Vermont. Though it was evening here in Paris, it was morning there. Would Suzie be awake?

Maybe this was a mistake, but he got the feeling Adelie wouldn't tell him if he came right out and asked. Suzie might have some idea of how he could approach the conversation he was hoping to have with Adelie.

She thought he still had feelings for Ruby; that wasn't the case at all. Ruby was a viper. Duncan hadn't been kidding about the risk she'd pose to Adelie if they were ever in the same room. Maddox truly had been trying to keep his word to Adelie, that he would protect her.

It'd been the reason he'd drawn away to have the conversation with Ruby earlier. He'd known how Ruby would argue with him when he asked her to back off and mind her own business. He'd finally ordered her to back off and ended the call, only to turn and find Adelie had vanished from the bridge.

Suzie could help him. She'd seemed peppy and friendly. Most of all, something told him she would be open to anything that would help Adelie, which was all he wanted. Impulsively, he dashed into the hall, to make sure Adelie didn't overhear the call.

"Hello?" Suzie's answer was bright and perky.

"Hey, Suzie, this is Maddox. Do you have a minute?"

"Sure. Good morning! Or I guess evening there. What's up?"

Maddox wasn't sure how to bring it up. He shared a little bit of the connection he'd been having with Adelie, careful not to disclose too much.

"But I can't seem to get close to her. She doesn't trust easily, does she?"

The other end of the line was quiet long enough, he thought she'd hung up on him. "Okay," Suzie finally said as if on an exhale. "Adelie will kill me if I tell you everything, but I'm going to tell you enough to help you get her, okay?"

"Okay," he said, unexpectedly unsure he wanted to hear whatever it was.

"Did Adelie tell you we were raised by our grandparents?" Suzie asked.

"She did. She said it was one reason she wanted to save their house."

"Yep. Did she tell you why?"

Maddox thought it over, trying to recall a conversation where the why had been mentioned. "She's closed off about it, but she did say they abandoned you when you both were young," he said. "And that her best memories were in your house."

"Maddox." Suzie's tone was solemn. "Our dad was abusive.

Not sexual. Just physical, but it was enough. Mom left him, left us, during the worst of it, and then they got in a car accident and passed away."

"Oh my gosh," Maddox said, stricken at the sound of the words.

"Yeah, it wasn't pretty for a while there. Finally, our grandparents intervened and got us out of a bad situation. If she's having a hard time trusting you, don't take it too hard. It's not you. I'm sure you're a decent guy. She just took it so hard, she was so young, you know? When it all happened."

"How old was she?"

"Seven," Suzie said. "She was seven when we left my dad and moved in with Grandma and Grandpa Carroll. Our lives were so much better, but I was able to forgive, let go, and move on much quicker than Addy was. Just give her time. Let her tell you her story and follow her lead."

"Wow," Maddox said, speechless. What did a person say to news like that? "Suzie, I'm so sorry that happened to you both."

It explained so much. Why Adelie hated being in the spotlight. Why she hated crowds, why she seemed so hesitant to let him touch her, to accept his compliments or assurances. There were times when he said or did things, and he sensed her pull away.

Mostly, it explained why she'd taken his actions so hard today when all he'd done was answered a different woman's phone calls—at Adelie's request, no less.

He didn't know much about helping someone overcome the results of an abusive situation, but he was certain about one thing. He wanted Adelie to trust him, to feel safer with him than she'd ever felt in her life. He wanted to help her heal.

A delie tossed and turned, fighting away tears the entire night. She was so messed up. Why couldn't she just let go of the past, of every insecurity that had stuck with her since her childhood? Her body had grown and lengthened as she'd grown into adulthood. Her face had matured, showing years of change from the babyish roundedness it had once had. She'd *changed* on the outside. Why couldn't her soul keep up the pace?

She knew Maddox wasn't like her father. Her brain knew it, anyway. Her heart was the tortoise in this race, unlike her hare brain, so quick to make judgments and bad calls. She'd tried for so long to keep herself shut away, locked safe in her grandparents' home, but here she was, on billboards and touring France, of all places. She was seeing the world. The world was seeing her.

And that was okay, wasn't it?

Not every encounter she had with people was going to be like those men in the grocery store. Not every man was like they were, like her father had been. Maddox was proof of that. She needed to let go, to let him in, to be okay with the choices she'd made recently instead of fighting them so much they were flaring up her anxiety.

So what if Maddox got a phone call from another woman. She needed to shift her focus. She needed to talk to Suzie.

Though it was late here, she dialed her sister's number. "What is going on with you two?" Suzie demanded the minute she answered.

"Um—what? What are you talking about?"

"I got off the phone with your husband not too long ago."

Adelie's jaw set. "Why did you call Maddox?"

"I didn't call him," Suzie said with a laugh. "He called me because he wanted to know how to reach you."

Adelie's jaw dropped. "He—he did?"

"Yes. He is seriously into you, Addy. If I didn't know any better, I'd say that husband of yours is falling in love with you. He wants to help you. To be close to you."

Falling in love with her? Adelie's stomach clenched. Her breathing turned shallow. She wasn't sure what to think. "What do you mean he wants to help me?"

"I told him about Dad," Suzie said, straightforward as always.

Shock overtook her. Enough time had passed that the memories that used to plague her didn't lambast her like they once did. Even the pain of those memories had faded unless she really focused on them. Which she chose not to at all costs.

"You did what? He doesn't need to know that, Suz. I'm a big enough wreck as it is without throwing our past into the mix."

"He's your husband," Suzie argued. "He should know the nitty gritties about you, if you guys want any kind of relationship."

"I'm not so sure he wants a relationship." Hard as she tried, she couldn't get past the way he refused to talk to his ex-fiancé in Adelie's company and instead took the call at a far enough distance away he didn't notice her leaving.

"Clearly, he does. Now the question is, what are you going to do about it?"

Could she believe it? Did he really want to be closer to her? To have an actual relationship with her instead of a protective, bodyguard kind of a marriage?

"Let him in," Suzie encouraged. "You never know. You might get hurt. Or you might hit the jackpot like I did with Fletcher."

Adelie wished she could hug her sister. "Thanks, Suz."

"You're in the most romantic city in the world. Look at all the things he's done for you, not all the ways it could go wrong. Remember the good and discard the rest. You can't go through life focusing on the ways people might let you down. He's already done so much to prove all of this to you, Adelie. Don't betray yourself out of fear."

Suzie's final words resounded like a battle cry in her mind.

Don't betray yourself out of fear.

Hindsight widened to become panoramic in her mind's eye. She'd been so stupid. Suzie was right—Maddox had done so much for her. He'd shown her only kindness. Even in moments of frustration, like with his ex calling, like when she'd left him on the bridge, Maddox had kept his temper. He hadn't lost control of himself like her father would have done.

He'd put his entire life on hold to protect her. The reality of that slammed into her with sudden force.

"Oh, my goodness," Adelie said. If she wasn't careful, she could push him away, and that was the last thing she wanted.

But she couldn't just let every barrier she'd built down at once.

"You know I'm right, don't you?" Suzie said smugly.

"Suzie, you're the best. And I have to go."

"Yep. You do."

"Bye, Suzie. Thank you so much."

Adelie's sudden optimism was off-putting. It didn't match how forlorn she'd felt for the better part of the evening. She shook her head, hoping Maddox wouldn't fault her for the whiplash of emotions she was dealing with. She also hoped he was still awake. Steadying her breathing, she opened the door.

Maddox's couch-bed was pulled out and roughly made. He sat against his pillow, in the dark, staring at the Eiffel Tower's sparkling majesty through the window. It glittered and gleamed like nothing Adelie had ever seen before.

"Maddox?" she said gently.

He peered back at her.

She took another step toward him. "I hope this comes out

okay, but can I stay with you in here tonight? Just to be close? I don't want to be alone, and—" She wrung her hands. "And I think it might be good for us to talk."

Wordlessly, he offered her a hand, and she took it, sinking onto the mattress beside him.

"It's really stunning, isn't it?" he said, returning his attention to the Eiffel Tower.

"It is." She was mesmerized by its fantastic sparkle, by its ability to point upward and shine with never-ending confidence. Adelie knew it was only a building, but in her current mood, a deeper insight struck her. In a strange way, she saw herself reflected in it.

It was almost as if, with every new glow, the Eiffel Tower gave Adelie permission to be a light as well. To be herself—her real self—no matter who she was around.

Maddox's arm slid around her, and she nestled into his side, allowing her head to rest against his shoulder. In the warmth of his embrace, the proximity, and prodded on by his heartbeat, Adelie saw herself in that magnificent structure.

She was different. Meant to stand out and be beautiful. She didn't want the praise of others, but it was okay for her to be seen. To glitter and gleam, to be unrelentingly herself.

"I keep thinking about you on Wonderland's brand. I really do think you're the perfect Alice," he said.

"You saw something in me that I didn't see in myself."

He faced her, brushing her knee with his. A hand stroked her cheek. "I only saw what everyone else has. What I want you to see too. That you are amazing and special. That you deserve every good thing life has to offer."

Keeping his hand around her, he lowered himself to the pillow beside the darkened, open window. Adelie's muscles were supple and willing. She lowered herself to face him, resting at his side, keeping her ear to his chest to hear the steady thrum of his heartbeat.

Maddox cradled her hand in his near his sternum as he rubbed soothing circles along her back. "Suzie told me about your dad." His voice was calm.

She nestled in closer. He was so safe, the safest she'd ever felt before. She liked his company, the assurance of his arm around her, of his masculine, no-nonsense voice rumbling in his chest. He gave her the sense that no matter what happened, she could face it with him.

"I know. She told me."

He rotated, resting his hand at her waist and lying on his side beside her. His feet tangled with hers at the bottom of the bed. Darkness looked good on him. It accentuated the line of his jaw and nose, deepening the intensity and softness in his eyes, which stared directly into hers as though nothing else existed.

"And you're okay with me knowing?"

Adelie scooted away. She'd never lain this close to a man before, and this man was her *husband*. "I am. Everything happened so fast between us, I—I don't know. I guess it never came up."

"I'm not sure there's any easy way to share something like that with anyone," he said. "You didn't owe me the explanation, but I'm glad I know."

She propped her head onto her elbow. "You are? Why?"

"Because I feel like I finally understand. I want you to know I'm a good person, Adelie. I—" He closed his eyes. "The idea that anyone could do what your dad did to you boils my blood. I wish I could take that away from you. I want you to know I'd never—*never*—do that to you. Or to our kids."

Adelie blinked. "Our—kids?"

"You know. Should we have any."

The warm cocoon that had settled around them burst.

Adelie sat up. She wasn't sure how to process her confusion. "Then you—you're saying you want this to be a permanent thing between us?"

He sat up too, resting his weight on one hand. "I think it's something we can talk about. I'm open to that. What about you?"

"I—I don't know."

"What *do* you want from me, Adelie?"

She looked directly at him, ready to be her bold, new self. "I want you to mean what you say."

"I do."

"How..." Her voice broke. "How can I believe you?"

"Why don't you?"

"You've been pushing me away since we said our vows. There have been moments between us where I think you're genuinely into me, but then right when I think we have a connection, you push me away."

She needed to be blunt. They had to have this out.

"I'm sorry," he said, brushing a lock of hair away from her face. She gazed into his night-shrouded eyes, and the gleam there shouted with sincerity.

"After the way those men treated you in Coleman's, I was trying to show you I would never force anything on you. I never meant to hurt you."

His admission circled in her chest like steam rising from a warm mug of cocoa. Her joints melted like wax.

He scooted closer. "I think I know a way that might convince you that you can trust me. I want to take things slow. But being here with you now, having you this close to me and seeing the way shadows are dancing on your skin, makes me want to kiss my bride."

"Maddox." Her voice was as weak as the rest of her body.

"I promise, I won't push you to go farther than you're ready to. If you're not up for that, then I just want you in my arms. But I think sometimes kisses have a way of speaking to the heart in a way nothing else can."

"You're not saying this because I'm your Alice, are you?"

He scooted closer still. His hand slid to her waist, and he pulled her onto his lap. Adelie gasped at being this close to him, being held by him in the darkness, having him touch her so intimately and look at her with such desire.

"You'll always be my Alice," he whispered. "But I'd want you even if you weren't."

She didn't protest this time but, instead, sensed every sliver of movement he made as he inched toward her. The way his heat radiated through her frame. The press of his chest against hers. The beat of his heart, the pulse of his fingertips on her jaw, gentle, so gentle. The last-minute gleam in his gaze and the moment his eyes closed just before his warm breath struck her, before his lips parted just enough, the perfect distance, to fold themselves over hers.

Their soft feel ignited awareness across her entire body. His arms tightened around her, enfolding her in a layer of safety and desire. The kiss was deliberate and slow and ended too soon before he pulled away to gauge her reaction.

She met his every glance, and he took it as the invitation it was. His head angled, his hand slid up to her neck, and he guided her back to his mouth, kissing her more insistently this time. Every motion was a flutter in her chest, a spark in her mind, and a promise. It seeped in a trickle at a time, until it filled her to the brim. She was wanted. She was safe. He'd meant what he'd said—he was like no other man she'd ever met.

Gradually, the kiss slowed, and she sat on his lap, cradled close to him, as they watched the Eiffel Tower continue its glistening, silent lullaby.

"Now do you believe me?" Maddox said moments later.

She rested her head against his shoulder. "I don't want to be alone tonight."

She wanted as much of his attention as she could get. She wasn't ready to consummate anything—that kiss was enough for now. Baby steps, just like Maddox had said.

Rather, she yearned for the emotional support he was giving her. She'd never experienced anything like this. It wasn't just the kiss. It was the promise that he was there for her. He was the shoulder she could lean on for support. And she wanted to be that for him too.

Maybe this was what love—what marriage—was all about. Being there for one another, in whatever way the other person needed.

"Then stay," he said, holding her once more. Just holding her. And it was perfectly enough.

———————

22

Sunlight gave gentle nudges to Adelie's subconscious. Her body was warm and heavy, comfortable and relaxed in every way it could be. The blanket covering her, the pillow beneath her head, Maddox's arm around her...

Maddox's arm...

Her eyes shot open. She clasped her hands to her chest, frozen. His warm, strong hand rested on her stomach, while his soothing breath stroked the back of her neck. Memories of their conversation—of their kiss—from the night before flurried around her like a snowstorm, though they were anything but cold.

Maddox Hatter, billionaire owner of Wonderland Theme Park, had kissed her. She'd had her first kiss, with a guy more amazing than she could have ever hoped for.

And she had fallen asleep in his arms.

Disbelief overwhelmed her. She rolled slightly to her side, praying the motion wouldn't wake him, and took advantage of his slumber to examine every inch of his handsome face.

His long lashes brushed chiseled cheekbones. Slight signs of aging lined his tanned forehead and near his eyes, just enough to be brushstrokes on an otherwise perfect canvas. She wasn't sure how old he was; in his thirties, she would guess.

His lips parted, and Adelie found herself entranced by their shape, by their fullness and the memory of how they'd felt against hers. Invisible hands guided her nearer, tempting her to press a new kiss there now, a surprise kiss. A morning kiss.

Adelie hovered, allowing the image to faze her before she thought better of it. Overcome with emotion, she slipped carefully free of his lax embrace and tiptoed to her own room. The floor creaked, and she winced, hurrying to close the door so she could have her own space to process everything that had happened.

Sinking onto the bed, she stared at everything and nothing while her heart chugged in her chest. What was going on here? She'd never felt this way for anyone. This stirring newness, the sense that a version of herself was surfacing, one that could only be accessed by Maddox and would only be truly seen by him.

She was lighter inside, fairly flying with all the excitement of it, with the realization that, at least for a moment, she'd been precious, wanted, and loved.

Carefully, slowly, she lifted a hand and stroked her bottom lip. Her mind couldn't completely make sense of how such a thing as a kiss could manage to imprint itself into everything she was, the direction of her blood flow and the strength in her muscles. It was artistic, the way it took the mold of her and reshaped her completely, into someone brighter. Was a kiss like this every time?

She had to talk to Suzie.

Morning Suz, she texted. *Any crazy men attack last night?*

Hundreds. Boyfriend did kung fu. You should have seen it. Of course, the house is a wreck now. There'll be no living here after this.

Adelie laughed as her hair swooped and created a curtain

between her and the window. She hugged the phone to her chest.

That's okay, she replied to Suzie. *I'm not sure I'll ever leave now that I'm here.*

Paris is everything you dreamed it would be?

That and more, Adelie replied, knowing there was no way to tell her just how much.

She started to text Suzie about her adventure the night before. Her romantic conversation with her new husband, the way Maddox had held her like an exquisite jewel, the way his lips had felt like the velvet skin of a peach against hers.

This wasn't something she could send in a text. It was extraordinary, breakable, not meant to be thrust out without care the way the rest of their playful conversation was.

She'd tell Suzie the next time she saw her.

Adelie decided to get dressed. Where before she would have just thrown on the first thing her fingers found in her suitcase, now, she flipped through what she'd packed, selective about her attire more so than she'd ever been for any job interview.

She opted for a coral shirt with khaki pants. After talking to herself in the mirror for several minutes, she mastered the nervous hammering in her chest and opened the door.

Maddox was sitting up in bed, skimming through something on his phone. Adelie slowed. She'd been caught staring and didn't mind in the slightest. In fact, Maddox seemed just as pleased to see her.

"Morning," he said, blinking at her. Was he wondering why she wasn't still with him? "You look incredible."

Blushing, Adelie ran a hand over her hair. "So do you."

He laughed and offered a hand in her direction. "Come here."

Adelie treaded toward him, preparing to settle on the bed's end. When he didn't lower his hand, she followed his lead, not stopping until her hand was in his and he cradled her against his chest.

"Did you sleep well?" he asked.

His smell of musk and sleep numbed her. "I did. Thank you for last night," she added. "You don't know how much I needed that."

"Are you talking about that kiss? Because that's all I've been able to think about since I woke up."

She chuckled. "That was...Yes. I guess that's part of it. You were my first kiss."

Maddox pulled away so he could look at her. "You're kidding, right?"

Her timidity threatened to take center stage, but she brushed it aside. "I'm really not. It was so special. It was like I was sharing my soul with you, and you saw me for who I really am. And that you're still okay with that."

Setting aside the blanket they'd shared, he rose from the bed and stopped before her, tipping her face to meet his. "I am. And once I brush my teeth, I'd like to kiss you again."

She giggled, whacking him with a pillow.

"Hey," he said. Defensively, he gripped her wrists. She giggled again, wriggling, attempting to free herself from his grasp. He bowled her over onto the pull-out bed, and the two of them tangled in the blankets like birds in a nest when his phone on the table beside it buzzed.

Freed from Maddox's grasp, Adelie rolled over and inspected the screen. All at once, the morning's elation died. Ruby's lovely, pouty expression filled his screen.

"She's calling you again," Adelie said. "What did you say to her when you answered yesterday? Did you tell her you're with me?"

Maddox scowled and reached for his phone. "Not yet. I'm just not sure how. Ruby can be a little territorial."

Adelie sat up. "Even if you aren't her territory anymore?"

Or was he? All of his playfulness and affection the past few days had to mean something. He couldn't be acting this way when he was still involved with someone else, could he?

"I'm going to answer this. I can go in the other room, if you want."

She didn't want to seem any more insecure than she already had, though inside, Adelie cringed.

"It's okay," she said, praying that it would be.

Maddox grimaced, wishing he could take the call somewhere Adelie wouldn't hear. But he wouldn't push her away again, not after the connection they'd had last night and then again this morning. Unlike Adelie, he'd kissed plenty of girls, but he wasn't sure there had ever been a kiss like that one. So tender, so vulnerable. It'd had a supercharged effect, like their exteriors had been stripped away and their souls had been connecting. Who knew a kiss could hold that much impact?

"Ruby," he said. "I asked you yesterday not to call me anymore. You ended things. Two years ago, in fact. It's time to move on."

Even as he spoke, he could sense Adelie distancing herself from him. He reached for her hand, latching it with his, and gave her what he hoped was a reassuring smile. Her shoulders lowered, and she returned the expression.

"Duncan told me an interesting bit of news," Ruby said, ignoring Maddox's comment. "Is it true you married this girl? Your Front-Page Girl?"

Defensiveness flared inside of him. That made Adelie sound cheap. "That's not your business anymore, is it?"

"There's nothing wrong with me wanting to congratulate an old friend on his sudden and unexpected marriage, is there?" Ruby's voice was an odd mix of sweetness, hissing tones, and sharp edges.

Maddox tried to figure out what spurred her snark. Why should Ruby care who he was with now, unless...

No way. She couldn't possibly be jealous. *She'd* been the one to end things, and she'd done it in the nastiest way possible.

"There wouldn't be if you actually meant it," Maddox said.

"I do mean it. Your little theme park is really taking off, and you're celebrating in the best way possible. Honeymoon and all."

"Goodbye, Ruby," Maddox said. This conversation was obviously going nowhere. He didn't want Ruby invading this amazing memory any more than she already had.

"And in France, no less," she went on. "I'm sure all your new fans will want to know your exciting news."

Maddox closed his eyes, regretting he'd ever answered the call the day before. He'd confessed where he was, hoping it would be enough to get Ruby off his case.

"If they do, it will be when Adelie and I are ready to announce it. Not before, you got it?"

"Keeping it to yourself? Where's the fun in that? This is the best marketing gimmick you've had yet. Marrying your model? People are going to gobble this up."

Maddox gritted his teeth and stood, releasing Adelie's hand in the process. "Hang on a second, Ruby. You're going too far."

She laughed, a wicked, familiar sound. "Oh, come on, don't tell me you actually have feelings for this girl. Didn't you just meet her at the rabbit event? The one I told you to do?"

He closed his eyes, praying for patience. He should have known she'd take credit for that. But she couldn't twist this; he refused to let her. His marriage to Adelie wasn't a marketing scheme. If anything, it was starting to feel like something he wasn't ready to say goodbye to anytime soon.

He decided to cut to the chase. "What is this really about?"

"I want in."

"What?"

"On your park. Make me an investor too."

This wasn't just unbelievable. This was asinine. Did she forget what she'd said so easily? Maddox had begged for her support when his park was struggling, when he'd really needed it, but she'd shot him down more times than he could count.

She couldn't be doing this now. Adelie was trying to stay out of the public eye. She was just starting to trust him. What would she do if she thought he'd married her to further his own interests?

"Stay out of this, Ruby. I mean it. I've moved on. You need to do the same."

"You never move on from money," Ruby said, ending the call and leaving Maddox with a sour pit in his stomach.

He wasn't sure what had just happened, but when it involved Ruby and her tenacity to land the best business deals possible, he wouldn't put anything past her.

23

Adelie wasn't ready to go home yet, which was funny, considering how a few days before she wanted to scamper away and hide. Now she wanted every moment alone with Maddox she could manage.

He'd changed, though, since Ruby's latest phone call. Something she'd said had put him off, though Adelie couldn't tell what.

"We should probably head back," he said as they'd shared ice cream cones in a little shop down the street. "I'd like to get you to my security again, as soon as possible."

Adelie licked the tip of her vanilla cone. *Get back* didn't mean to their hotel. He meant returning to Vermont. "What does that mean? Did Ruby say something to you?"

His smile seemed too forced. "No, it's just that I don't think we should stay too much longer. Better to be safe than sorry."

"Sorry for what?" Being in Paris? This had been the best trip of her life. It didn't hurt that Maddox continued stealing kisses on street corners and bridges.

Maddox tipped his ice cream toward her. "That's just it. We don't know, so we'd better head back."

Later, while back in their room, he spent some time on the phone with someone named Rosabel, whom Adelie discovered was Duncan's assistant who'd arranged their trip in the first place. From the sound of things, they were set to depart for Vermont the following day.

Maddox ended the call and turned to face her.

"Leaving so soon?" Adelie added a pout for good measure.

Amused, Maddox scooped her into his arms. "I think I'd stay here with you longer if we could. You should know I think Ruby has something up her sleeve. I'd rather be on home base, to have you within my security's protection in case of whatever it is."

"You can't think she'd actually do anything to me." Adelie's dismay was genuine. He'd called Ruby territorial. Would Ruby come at Adelie physically?

"No, not to you personally. It's just that, she implied..."

"Implied what?"

His brow pinched. "Nothing. It may not even happen. But there is one thing I'd like to do before we leave Paris."

"Oh?" Her thoughts tangled into knots. So many possibilities could fit that particular description.

He wove his fingers through hers and gave her an endearing grin. "Yes. Get your shoes on, Mrs. Hatter. We're going for a walk."

≈

Maddox talked easily of memories of his first visit to Paris with his family as a teen, and of the time he'd eaten ice cream on the bridge while they'd waited for the sun to set and the Eiffel Tower to flare to life.

"Where are we going?" Adelie asked, completely flummoxed and dying of anticipation. She had to know what he had up his sleeve.

"You'll see."

They rounded a corner to a row of picturesque shops. Adelie wasn't sure she'd ever acclimate to the architecture in this city. Haussmanian stone buildings with wrought-iron railings and stained glass seemed like the epitome of class, and they were everywhere.

"Here we go." Maddox gestured to a store bearing the title *Chez Mercier Bijoux*. Tall glass windows displayed delicate, sparkling necklaces on dainty stands, set off by black velvet. So much sparkle in one window almost put the Eiffel Tower to shame. Almost.

"A jewelry store? What are we doing here?"

Maddox smirked. Pinning his gaze on hers, he lifted her left hand and kissed a certain, bare finger. "I just wanted to make our marriage official. I didn't ever give you a ring."

Adelie's hand lingered in his. He couldn't be serious. "Maddox, that means—you know what a ring means, right?"

"Commitment," he said. "I know this marriage of ours has been completely backward and inside out from the start, but I'm of the opinion it's never too late to set things right. I'd like you to feel secure about me, in case…"

"In case what?"

A thought bothered him. He shook it away and smiled. "Nothing. I just want you to have a ring. You deserve a ring."

Adelie stared, flabbergasted. Was he serious?

She didn't voice the question aloud, and he didn't answer with words. Instead, he brought his lips to hers, spearing heat all the way through the empty spaces inside of her. The gleam in his eyes said more than anything he ever could. How could he look at her like that? Like she was the only woman who'd ever existed?

"What do you say?" he said, his voice low.

She managed to find her voice. "Yes. I'd love a ring from you."

He kissed her once more and opened the door.

The displays were blinding. Adelie examined each carefully, receiving gentle nudges and tickling strokes from Maddox whenever he caught her staring too long at anything but him.

She didn't want anything too gaudy. Just something simple and perfect, unassuming and plain, the way she wanted to be viewed. Maddox tried to talk her into a larger carat, but she insisted on something small. She was the one who'd be wearing it, after all. Not him.

"This one," she finally said, admiring its fit on her hand. It was a thin, white-gold band, accented by a square diamond and paired with a diamond-plaited wedding band so it looked as though she wore two rings with one jewel.

"It's perfect," Maddox said as the jeweler took it to the back to be sized to her slim fingers. Adelie was thrilled when Maddox agreed on wearing the corresponding men's band.

The next day, after they retrieved the rings, Maddox slid hers onto her finger. With the new addition, her hand seemed to make its way out in front of her everywhere she went. She admired its gleam as she took in the sight of her hand twined with Maddox's in the car on the way to the airport. She admired it on his plane as they shared kisses on the luxurious leather couch and eventually fell asleep together for the long flight home. And she admired it after they made it back to Vermont and through Maddox's security to his generously sized home.

Somehow, the ring made things that much more secure for her. He wouldn't have bought one for her—and for himself—if he didn't want this relationship of theirs to remain as it was.

She still felt uncertain and wanted things out in the open. She wanted to know exactly how he felt. Exactly how long he wanted to be married to her for, because the way things were going, she never wanted it to end.

Maddox knocked on her door the next morning. She was too distracted by the sight of the ring on her finger to manage studying much, though she was doing her best to learn the confusing, medical prefixes and suffixes for her terminology class. At this rate, and with him around, she'd never pass her upcoming exam.

She opened the door only to find herself bundled into his arms and thoroughly held.

"Good morning," he said into her neck. He suspended her against him the way a dancer in a routine might, staring up at her with complete satisfaction.

"Good morning," she said with a grin.

"I had a thought." He lowered her to stand on her feet. "And you don't have to—I mean, it doesn't have to be more than, well —I mean, we are married."

She chewed her bottom lip. "You're cute when you're tongue-tied."

Color flushed his cheeks, but he didn't release her. "I'm just saying, I miss you."

"You do?"

"Yeah. You know, you're all the way in here. And I'm all the way in my room."

He indicated its direction with his head. In a house as large as his, it did seem like there was a league between them.

"I just wondered if you might want to share my room with me. Like we did in Paris. It doesn't have to be anything more than that. Not unless you want it to be."

"Maddox." She didn't know what to say.

He was right—they were man and wife. Would it be so bad? The truth was, she missed him too. She was having a harder and harder time concentrating on school or answering Suzie's texts or dealing with anything else but him.

"You don't have to answer now. Just think about it, okay?" He kissed her, and she melted on the spot. "Anyway, I wanted to let you know, I've got to head into Wonderland today. Do you want to come with me?"

The offer tempted her, but it wasn't enough to brush aside her pressing exam that was just a few more days away.

"I'd better not," she said. "I've got a test soon, and I'll never pass this class if I don't get some studying done."

This time, he did the pouty lip.

"Better be careful with that," she said, tiptoeing up to kiss him.

"Get your studies done," he said. "I'll see you for dinner tonight, okay?"

She was becoming more and more of a puddle the longer he stayed. "Okay. I'll miss you."

He grinned and was gone.

Adelie settled in. She forced her mind to focus, though she couldn't stop thinking about his offer. Had he really asked her to share a room with him? She didn't want to consider all the implications, so she did her best to concentrate.

After lunch, she relocated to the expansive front room, eager to soak in its comfortable arrangement of furniture and the sun spattering through the massive windows. Music helped her concentrate, and she was so caught up in terms and phrases, she almost missed the doorbell's ring.

Adelie glanced up. Kirk was nowhere in sight, so she laid down her books and made her way to the door, opening it without a thought. Chances were, it was Maddox with a bouquet of flowers or some other crazy, romantic gesture. That seemed like the kind of thing he might do.

It wasn't Maddox. A perky blonde woman Adelie recognized —carrying a microphone and backed by a cameraman— beamed at her.

"Hey, there. It's Adelie, right?" She jutted out her hand. "Wendy Hendricks. You may remember, we met the day you found Mr. Hatter's rabbit."

"I—yes, I remember." The unpleasant memory was a splash against a newly finished watercolor. In an instant, the happy, swirling, comforting image she'd painted for herself in her mind began to muddy and ebb into an incomprehensible mash.

Adelie wanted to retreat, to shut the door. Was Wendy recording her now? How had she gotten past security? Did Maddox arrange this?

Wendy lowered her hand. "Some rumors have flown recently, between you and Mr. Hatter, and I thought I'd see if I could ask you a few questions."

Rumors. Had word of their marriage leaked? Or maybe it was their trip to Paris.

"I'd rather not." Adelie motioned, trying to figure out a nice way to uninvite this woman from the doorstep. While she was married to Maddox, this still didn't seem like *her* house. Could she demand she leave?

"Oh my gosh, is that a ring?" Wendy flagged her cameraman. "Miss Carroll, are the rumors true? Did you and Mr. Hatter get married?"

"I'm not answering anything. Sorry." Adelie nearly succeeded at closing the door before a separate hand shot out.

"Come on, that's no way to treat this nice lady."

The woman Adelie had only seen on Maddox's phone strutted up from behind Wendy. She wore a skin-tight, floral dress that cut short at the thigh, and the tallest heels Adelie had ever seen. Her dark hair fell in thick waves past her shoulders.

Adelie's defenses went onto high alert. Ever since her childhood, she'd had a sense about unsafe people, and Ruby triggered every one of her reservations in an instant. Her pushy manner. Her quick movement toward Adelie and lack of respect for Adelie's obvious discomfort.

Like Wendy, Ruby jutted out a hand in Adelie's direction. Against her better judgment, Adelie shook it.

"Pleased to meet you. I'm Ruby, and Maddsy told me all about you."

Maddsy?

Adelie's old anxieties trickled back in. The way her head blanked out. The way her pulse skyrocketed. The way she felt as though she'd been struck.

"I think you should go." Adelie's voice was weak. Too weak.

Ruby waved her off while beckoning Wendy and her cameraman on, into Maddox's foyer.

"We'll be fast friends," Ruby said. "Just like Wendy and me here. She just wants to ask you a few questions. No big deal, right?"

Flashbacks of the grocery store blanched Adelie's vision. She couldn't let this happen—she'd come here for safety, not to be cornered once more. She had to grow a backbone sometime. Maddox had married her. He'd invited her to not only live here, but to share his personal space. That had to mean something.

Adelie clenched her fists at her sides. She crammed energy into her voice in a way she never had before.

"No." Her lower lip began to tremble, along with her ribcage. She clenched her fists tighter and rammed the words out past her angst. "It is a big deal. I'm not answering anything and you —" Her voice broke. She forced it back. "I'm asking you to leave."

Ruby quirked a brow. She angled her jaw and folded her arms across her chest. Adelie waited for her to continue arguing, but to her relief, she turned to the news anchor.

"Go on," she ordered Wendy, who left with her cameraman without a word.

"You too," Adelie said, keeping her head high.

"So commanding," Ruby said. "But I'm not blind, sweetheart. I see the rock sparkling on your left hand, which means that beast, Duncan Hawthorne, was telling me the truth."

Adelie's arms went rigid. For a minute, she had the urge to hide her hand, but why should she? She had nothing to be ashamed of.

"What does it matter whether I'm wearing a ring or not?"

Ruby seemed to find this amusing. Smirking, she paced, just a few steps, back and forth across the foyer.

In an instant, Adelie got an image of the Red Queen from *Alice's Adventures in Wonderland* about to pronounce the unfortunate person in closest proximity was set to have his head removed.

Adelie wasn't sure how to get this woman to leave. She shot Maddox a hasty text before lowering her phone.

Ruby is here. Please come as quick as you can.

"That Maddsy. He played things so well with you."

"Excuse me?" Adelie didn't have to add spice to her tone. It was coming naturally now, matching Ruby's spitfire persona.

She chuckled and folded her arms over her chest, jutting out a single hip. "Oh, don't you worry. I'm sure you'll get a share too. After all, it's thanks to you his profits will triple after this story gets out."

"What are you talking about?"

Shock washed over her as Ruby's words became clear. Was she implying Maddox married her for publicity? Though Adelie had once suspected as much, she didn't believe it now. He couldn't have faked the emotion they'd shared in Paris. It couldn't be true.

Ruby tilted forward, took in the sight of Adelie's ring, and grunted. "Pity. Mine was bigger."

"Get out," Adelie snapped through her teeth, clutching her fist to her chest to hide the ring.

Ruby's perfect brow arched, and another smirk lifted the corners of her red lips.

"Don't tell me you thought this whole façade was real."

"Now."

Ruby cast her glance around before sighing. "Whatever." She pivoted and strutted out the front door, not bothering to close it behind her.

Tears distorted Adelie's vision, and while she was tempted to slam the thick door closed with all the energy she had, she closed it carefully, quietly, and returned to her room.

24

I t was no use. No matter how many times Maddox glanced at the clock, time wasn't going any faster. He might as well go back home. He was about as useful as a broken watch after his offer to Adelie this morning and the way he could feel her walls crumble.

She was letting him in. They were making progress as a couple; in a way he'd never anticipated when he'd suggested they marry for convenience's sake. He didn't want to be here at his stuffy office, no matter how much work he had left to do for the day. He wanted to be with her.

Maddox slipped into his suitcoat and headed for the door, but it opened before he reached it. He half expected a pair of Converse shoes to approach him, to lift his head and find Duncan sneering at him and bugging him for a round of golf to get away from his annoyingly attractive assistant—Duncan's words, not Maddox's.

But these shoes were pointed-toe alligators, green as envy and just as scaly. They led up to a form-fitted floral dress, hugging in all the right places and cutting short at the thigh. Ruby's face turned in a sneer as she folded her arms.

Maddox cursed himself for staring at her so long. Undoubtedly, she'd taken it for attraction rather than the repulsion coursing through him.

"I love it when I can make a man disoriented by my mere presence," Ruby said.

Her hair was as dark as her demeanor, flowing past her shoulders. Her lips were a rosebud to match her name, and the almond of her dark eyes narrowed further when he didn't reply.

"What are you doing here?" Had his receptionist allowed her back here? She knew better. Then again, Ruby had a way of getting around barriers, even when they were put up solely to keep her out.

Her shoes clacked on the tile as she strutted over and rested a hip against his desk. The lamp jostled. "Been seeing a lot of you lately. Or your park, anyway."

"I'm sure you have. I thought I told you on the phone, I'm done with you."

She examined a fingernail. "If I recall, there was a time you wanted me to see you. You wanted me to invest in your park, and in a life with you."

"That's funny," he said, shoulders hardening. "I seem to recall you telling me I wasn't worth the dirt Wonderland stood on. That the park would fail, and you didn't want to be around when it did."

"Ancient history." She lifted herself to sit on the desk, dislodging his pen cup in the process. Pens spilled across his papers and his closed laptop. Ruby gave them a fleeting glance as though they were just one more thing that'd been in her way.

"You still haven't told me what you're doing here." Maddox folded his arms. He didn't want to give her the impression she could throw her weight around like she used to. He hadn't minded then. In fact, he'd found it intriguing and attractive. Now he saw her for what she really was.

Careless and selfish.

She crossed one leg over the other. "I told you. I want in."

"No."

"I'm no fool, Maddox. I know a good thing when I see it. You hit the jackpot with your little wife. Your numbers have been skyrocketing, and you need me if you want to keep that momentum going."

He needed her? He'd done all of this *without* her.

"How could you possibly know what my numbers are doing?" Duncan wouldn't have told her. Beastly though his best friend could sometimes seem, Maddox refused to believe Duncan would sell him out, especially to Ruby. He knew their history as much as Maddox did.

Maddox didn't know what to say. Ruby was the reason he'd been seeking out investors for years after she pulled her backing from him. Right when he'd needed her the most.

He didn't need her now, nor did he need this. Although, he supposed it was good she'd come here to him rather than targeting Adelie. As long as Ruby stayed away from her, he could handle this.

Ruby removed herself from his desk and strutted toward him. He got a waft of her snake scent as she tiptoed in and pressed a kiss to his cheek. He attempted to pull back, but not soon enough.

"You know where to find me," she said, tucking something into his breast pocket and waltzing out.

Stunned, Maddox waited until she was gone to examine the business card. She'd changed her logo, but her name blared like a neon sign. *Ruby Regina. Investing Insights, Strategies, Services, and Solutions.*

"She should add a subheading," he said to his empty office as he crumpled her card and lobbed it toward the garbage can. "*Will backstab at first sign of failure.*"

It was amazing she still had a business if she treated all her clientele the way she'd treated Maddox. It probably didn't help that they'd been dating on top of their business relationship.

The scathing words she'd said to him the last time she'd been in this office had rubbed him raw for years. He'd done his best to push them aside, to push her aside and let go of the hurt they'd caused.

A failure. A washout. A desperate man with nothing. Her words had taunted him like bullies, and now she had the gall to not only offer to back the park she'd once called pathetic, but to kiss him on the cheek?

She *knew* he was married. She knew he was with Adelie. Maddox glanced at his phone, and his heart sank. It'd buzzed earlier, but he'd been on a phone call and hadn't checked the message. Now he wished he had.

"Oh no," Maddox said, dashing out the door.

Here, he'd thought he'd been Ruby's first stop, but like always, he should have known better. Ruby was a viper. She'd snag her teeth into any unsuspecting victim she could if it meant her own personal gain. She was going to ruin everything he'd built with Adelie. He had to get home as quickly as possible.

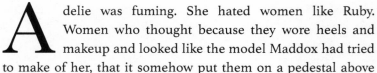

Adelie was fuming. She hated women like Ruby. Women who thought because they wore heels and makeup and looked like the model Maddox had tried to make of her, that it somehow put them on a pedestal above others.

The judgment and criticism in Ruby's expression had drifted off her like a stench, and it still permeated Adelie's thoughts and set a match to her blood.

"How dare she?" she said aloud.

What business was it of hers whether Adelie and Maddox were married or not? And what had she meant, about Maddox playing things properly?

Adelie stared at the ring she'd been so mesmerized by before, but it seemed to have lost some of its luster. The only thing that seemed clearer than glass was her own stupidity for ever trusting him.

"I should never have signed that contract," she spat to her suitcase, grateful yet again she hadn't completely unpacked it. "I should never have done the photo shoot, should never have agreed to this stupid..." Her strength broke. She rested her hands on the suitcase and lowered her head, choking back tears.

Footsteps hammered in the hall outside her door, and then it was flung open and Maddox stormed in. He drew her to him, but she pushed him away.

"Stop," she said.

"Ruby came here, didn't she? Adelie, I'm so sorry."

"Me too," Adelie said. "I'm sorry I fell for it. For you." She wished she had more things to slam into her suitcase. She rolled up her favorite blanket and hugged it to her chest, needing to hold onto something.

"What did she say to you?"

"Just that I'm nothing more than a pawn in your marketing scheme. So clever of you, to pretend to protect me only to sic her on me with a news crew." Granted, it wasn't a crew, but she was going for dramatics here.

"She what?"

Adelie sniffed. "It doesn't matter. I'm sure you'll see the story on tonight's broadcast."

"Adelie—I'm so sorry. I'll talk to Juan. She never should have been allowed through my security."

"She used to be allowed, though, right? So, he probably thought she was legit."

"I'm sorry," Maddox said again. "I didn't think—I should have spoken with him about her. I was just relieved to be back here."

Adelie's heart hardened. She couldn't keep crying like this. She couldn't let him affect her anymore. And most of all, she couldn't stay. "Guess it's good I never unpacked."

He winced. "I was hoping to have you unpack a little closer to me."

"Why, so you could have cameras there too?"

Maddox brow snapped down so fast, she sensed he was truly offended by her insinuation. Honestly, what else was she supposed to think? Just when she was starting to trust him.

"I'm serious." He turned her to face him. "I meant what I said this morning. You're important to me, Adelie. This—our marriage—wasn't a marketing gimmick."

Another tear leaked out. She wriggled free of his touch. "I knew better than to agree to any of this. I'm leaving."

"You can't," he said. "There will probably be cameras everywhere, if you say she got a story on you."

Adelie was fed up. She tossed her hands. "Then it's probably time I stop hiding and face up to it, don't you think? I need to learn how to some time. Might as well be now. Goodbye, Maddox." She pried off the ring and thrust it at his chest, carting her suitcase and the sting of his betrayal in her wake.

25

The news splashed on every channel and every front page in Vermont. Headlines blared, *Billionaire Marries His Model*; *Alice Hit the Jackpot: Marries Her New Boss,* along with unflattering pictures of Adelie in his house from the confrontation, and even several romantic shots of the two of them in Paris. Figures, that Ruby would have hired someone last minute to spy on them and take a few pictures.

Unless Maddox had told her exactly where they would be. Maybe that was the reason he'd been so hesitant to answer Ruby's calls while they'd been there. He hadn't wanted Adelie to overhear the scheme.

Adelie didn't want to wallow. She was tired of hiding; that was what had spurred this entire fiasco in the first place. Besides, what was the point? There wasn't anywhere she could go where her face wouldn't be in everyone else's.

She meandered through town, needing a new purpose. Her grandma had always said helping others during your distress was the best way of coping. If only she'd done that before, instead of hiding like a coward.

She hadn't been entirely certain where she was headed until her car slowed in front of Ella's apartment building. She and her cousin had been close friends throughout their childhood, but they'd grown apart as they'd grown up. Ella's complicated family situation hadn't helped matters, and neither had Adelie's shy, anxious tendency to withdraw from anyone with a pulse.

The apartment complex was squat and brick, with multiple levels and in need of drastic repairs. The fact that Ella was about to marry a billionaire wasn't as much of a shock to her as it was that moment, now that Adelie knew something about how the wealthy lived. Undoubtedly, Ella and Hawk's home would be like a palace compared to this place.

Adelie exited her car, locked the doors, and made her way to the glass door. Ella's apartment was on the third floor. Adelie climbed the stairs rather than taking the elevator, and she paused outside the door only a moment before knocking.

Ella answered as chipper as a bird in springtime. Her already smiling face lit up at the sight of Adelie.

"Hey!" she exclaimed. "What are you doing here? I heard the happy news. You decided to spread the word, huh?" Then, without giving Adelie a chance to answer, she reeled around and shouted over her shoulder. "Grammy! Charlotte! You'll never guess who's here."

Adelie's heart ticked like a clock. "Grandma Larsen is here?" Guilt swam over her. She hadn't spoken much with her mother's mom since she'd come to help clean Ella's apartment the Christmas before last.

"Come in, come and see my dress. You're going to die over this fabric." Ella yanked Adelie in, and the touch alone was a comfort.

"I—I came to see if you needed help."

"Pfft." Ella waved her off. "You already did so much. Come

hang out, tell us how newlywed bliss is working out for you." She added a wink as they made it past the hall that served as an entryway into a small dining and kitchen area.

Ella was notoriously cluttered. Even as girls, her room had always been messy. This mess wasn't the usual, however. Scads of white fabric covered every surface in the room. A small TV blared behind Ella, but Adelie couldn't see what it played through her grandma's all-encompassing hug.

"You got married and didn't tell me!" Grammy Larsen's tone carried a kind reprimand.

Adelie winced and lowered her eyes. Grammy Larsen tipped a finger to her chin and had such a happy sparkle in her eyes, Adelie knew she wasn't being scolded. Just teased.

"Congratulations."

"Thanks, but..."

Glancing around, the feeling that this had been the wrong place to come swept over her. Ella was floating on clouds, sky-high in love with her handsome catch. A man who had actually dated her, had gotten to know her and fallen in love with her. Truth stung her eyes, and she blinked hard.

Jabbering with her roommate and stepsister, Charlotte, Ella lifted what appeared to be the train of her wedding gown, gushing over the difficulty of sewing with lace and keeping the seams from cinching, when she glanced over.

Adelie's lower lip trembled. She slammed her eyes closed. Blast it all, this wasn't why she was here. She'd come to help, to try and forget. The last thing she needed was to spread her marital problems here when Ella was about to get married.

"What's wrong?" Grammy Larsen asked.

Adelie sank into a chair and plunged her head into her hands. Against her better judgment, the entire story spilled out, from being selected as Maddox's model for Wonderland, to the attack at Coleman's, to their rushed marriage and impromptu honeymoon. Finally, she shared Ruby's interference and the insinuations she'd made regarding Maddox's reasons for proposing marriage in the first place.

"That makes no sense whatsoever." Ella's anger ignited in her tone. Charlotte passed Adelie a tissue, as Grammy Larsen perched against the table, frowning in Adelie's direction. "I just can't believe he was using you the whole time."

Adelie sniffed and blew her nose. "I thought the same thing."

"Hogwash," Grammy said, startling the three younger women in the room.

Adelie wiped her cheeks. "What is?"

"If that man really used you to get his business ahead, then shame on him. He'll have to answer to God for fiddle-faddle like that—and to me, for that matter." Ella folded her arms and nodded her agreement. Adelie had no doubt Grammy would rush in and demand answers of Maddox for mistreating her the way he had.

Grammy slid a chair closer to Adelie, sat down, and took Adelie's hands in her soft ones. "But what do you think, Addy girl?"

Adelie nearly smiled at the old nickname her grandma had never stopped using for her, but she was still too distraught.

"Search deep down, in your inmost thoughts and heart. I'm not saying there aren't men out there who are scum and who do take advantage of women in all kinds of awful ways. And I'm not saying the women who get bamboozled by them can always tell it's happening. But that doesn't mean this Maddox of yours is one of them. You said you thought he cared for you?"

Her thoughts sprang to the kiss they'd shared while watching the Eiffel Tower through the darkened Paris night, of waking in his arms, of their flight home and how he hadn't been able to keep his distance from her, how he'd always had a hand on her knee or in hers even when they were the smallest distance apart. That hadn't seemed false.

Adelie's throat was too tight to speak, yet she somehow wrangled out the words.

"Yes. There were moments between us that felt so real." Not a dream. She wasn't going to wake from this. She'd had a connection with Maddox, one he couldn't have been faking.

"And you say you left before either of you could say much. After this Ruby butted her nose into your business."

Another nod.

Grammy Larsen patted her hand. "Then you know what you need to do."

"I do?" Adelie's gaze darted from Grammy's kind, wrinkled eyes to Ella's sweet countenance and Charlotte's fervent nod.

"Go talk to him," Ella interjected. "It's normal to have problems. Hawk and I had our first fight over how to cook spaghetti." She giggled as though it was ludicrous. "I know it doesn't compare to what you're going through, but you've got to talk to him. Hear what he has to say. Let him defend himself or plead guilty, but either way, he's the one you need to be working through this with."

A rock slid into her stomach, yet something else slid inside her with it. Something warm and encouraging. Something that told her she could do this. Maybe it was Grammy Larsen's gentle yet coaxing manner or Ella's helpful sweetness.

Adelie smiled through her tears. "And here I thought I'd come here to help you."

"Of course, you can help me," Ella chuckled, pulling her into a hug. "Just get home and talk to that husband of yours."

Home. Home had always been Grandma and Grandpa Carroll's house, but the first image flashing in her mind with the word was Maddox's. Could his home become hers after all?

True to her word, Adelie helped pin fabric and then held it

up to keep it from dragging on the floor as Ella guided it through her sewing machine. The friendly chatter and jokes about Hawk's uneasiness with airplanes and confined spaces and how Ella worried she'd have to drug her husband if she wanted to get him to take her on any kind of honeymoon, the prattle about Charlotte's boyfriend, and about how Grammy Larsen's job working at *Ever After Sweet Shoppe* had lasted longer than she'd planned on, but how she enjoyed sneaking treats every chance she could, warmed Adelie's heart.

Still, by the time she left, she wasn't ready to go back to Maddox's house. Her heart ached for the connection they'd shared while in Paris. Though Ella had called his mansion her home, Adelie wasn't sure where that was anymore.

～

"Would you hold still? You're making me dizzy."

Maddox hadn't been able to stay in one place. He'd hardly slept the night before. His final conversation with Adelie before she'd darted from his home had been a broken record in his mind ever since. How could he have ever let this happen?

Showing what a good friend he was, Duncan had come at Maddox's request, but he didn't get the chance to take Maddox's offer and sit down. Instead, he'd stood in front of the closed office door, jacket in hand, and gaped at him.

"You'd pace too if you'd just lost the love of your life," Maddox grumbled.

"The love of your life?" Duncan's tone was snider than usual. Maddox gave him a sidelong glance. While his friend was notoriously snappish at his own office, he wasn't usually that way here with him. Had something happened?

Duncan brushed something from the jacket in his hand. "I can't say I've ever had that pleasure."

Upon first arrival, Duncan had admitted he'd gotten into another spat with his assistant over something completely trivial. Seriously, how could booking flights be cause for an argument?

While Maddox's best friend had fired plenty of assistants in the past for lesser reasons—he'd fired one girl for spelling a name wrong on a company invitation, for goodness' sake—it wasn't like Duncan to complain this much about Rosabel and do nothing about it.

It gave Maddox a sneaking suspicion that the rumors Duncan also complained about—that something more between him and Rosabel was going on—were true. If that was the case, Maddox couldn't understand why Duncan wouldn't just admit he had feelings for his assistant.

"Forget it," Maddox said, regretting he'd invited Duncan over in the first place. He'd needed someone to talk to, though. Speaking with Duncan in person wasn't the respite he'd hoped for.

Duncan placed his jacket on the bar, crossed the room, and stopped Maddox with his hands on his shoulders. "Look. I'm sorry. I didn't know you liked her so much. I thought you—"

"I told you how I felt about her," Maddox argued. "Don't tell me you're taking Ruby's side in this."

"It was crazy rushed, man," Duncan said in his defense. "You just up and married her. How else is it supposed to look?"

Maddox shook his head. "I didn't care how it looked. It wasn't supposed to leak, not until we were ready."

"And now that it is, the whole world is going to think the same thing as Ruby."

"I have to do something," Maddox said, frustrated by the

entire turn of events. "She thinks this is all about the money for me."

"Ruby?"

"No," he snapped. "Adelie."

Duncan lifted his hands. "You mean it's not about the money?"

Maddox worked to keep his frustration in check. "No, and while we're on the subject, why did you tell Ruby at all? You're the one who warned me about getting Ruby involved."

Duncan shrugged. "When Ruby called me to find out where you were, I didn't answer. She talked to Rosabel instead. Then when she got a hold of me later, I assumed Ruby knew when she mentioned you were in Paris."

Maddox sank onto his couch and ran his hands through his hair. Relief seeped through some of his frustration. At least he knew Duncan hadn't betrayed him.

"Sorry," he said. "I'm just on edge from all of this. I know you're trying to help me."

Duncan inclined his head to one shoulder. "Don't get me wrong, I've got problems of my own. I'd get a fake wife myself if it hadn't turned out so rotten for you. Maybe that would get my staff to believe there's nothing going on between Rosabel and me."

The words struck Maddox. He wasn't about to confront Duncan about Rosabel again, not since he'd closed up about her so entirely the last time he'd tried.

"That's just it, though. Our marriage has been mind-blowing, the way she's so perfect for me, the way I feel like I'd do anything for her. Adelie is such a sweetheart. She makes me want to conquer the world for her—if it needed conquering. I don't want it to be over."

Duncan frowned at him. "Then what are you still doing here?"

"I don't know. I don't know how to prove it to her, how to prove I care about her and not the money." Thanks to Ruby, Wonderland was in the way. It'd been in the way since he'd met Adelie, when it started out as something good and beautiful he'd created in honor of his mother.

"You could always close Wonderland."

Duncan's words traveled to Maddox as if from a distance. The thought was so simple and obviously meant as another joke, but it struck a chord inside Maddox. Slowly, he rose to his feet and stared at his friend.

"You're a genius."

He held a palm toward him. "I wasn't being serious."

He glanced out the window of Maddox's office, which he'd purposefully located in the White Rabbit's house so he could take in the exhilaration of the park without anyone knowing he was there.

Unable to wipe the dawning smile from his face, Maddox strode over and clapped him on the back. "Can I borrow Rosabel's assistance again?"

"Rosabel?" Duncan said, as though he'd forgotten who she was.

"Yes," Maddox said with a laugh. Rosabel, the one everyone in Duncan's office thought Duncan was having an illicit relationship with when really the two could hardly stand to be in the same room together.

Maddox still wasn't sure why Duncan hadn't found a different assistant, one who would suit him better. He had to have feelings for her.

"You sure she won't mind taking care of a few things for me?" Maddox asked.

Duncan paused before his lips twisted against a smile. "She won't mind. She loves doing extra work." His tone gave Maddox the impression the opposite was true.

Maddox retreated from the idea. Rosabel had helped him out a lot the past few weeks, and he didn't want to make her feel unappreciated.

He surrendered his hands. "You know what? Never mind. I don't want to bother her."

"No, please," Duncan said too eagerly. He tapped his screen. "She *loves* to be bothered."

Maddox opened his mouth to protest when a woman's voice could be heard through Duncan's phone.

"Hey, there, Assistant. My buddy has a request for you."

Maddox didn't like it. How could Duncan treat her this way? How could Rosabel put up with it?"

Sneering, self-satisfied, Duncan offered him his phone. Reluctantly, Maddox took it

"Hey, there, Rosabel."

"Hey, Mr. Hatter," Rosabel said sweetly. Was she annoyed? She hadn't been when she'd coordinated his honeymoon at the last minute. Maddox should have considered her feelings more carefully.

"I'm sorry to bother you again. You did a fantastic job with my accommodations in Paris. I just wanted to thank you."

"Oh?" Her tone turned shrewd. "Would you please tell Mr. Hawthorne how nice it is to hear those words once in a while?"

Maddox froze with the feeling he'd landed himself in some kind of battle between the two of them. A battle he was sure he wanted nothing of. As Duncan had said, he had his own problems right now.

He cleared his throat awkwardly. "Yes, well, that's all I wanted to say."

"Sorry," she said, sounding exasperated and repentant. "I shouldn't talk to you like that." She cleared her throat as well and then her tone brightened. "Mr. Hawthorne said you had something to ask me?"

Maddox grimaced. He could take care of this himself. Or hire his own assistant. He didn't have time for that, though. Truly, he needed Rosabel's help. Maddox spilled his idea, reassuring himself that he'd make it worth her while.

26

A delie stared at her medical terminology course page.
The test results were in, and hers were unbelievable.
A ninety-three percent? Even after how muddled
she'd felt after things with Maddox when everything capsized,
even when she hadn't been able to think as clearly as usual,
she'd still managed to remember everything she'd studied?

She could live without him after all. That was evident from
the results of her test.

But she didn't want to.

Her conversation with Ella and Grammy Larsen clamored
through her mind. She wanted to follow their advice, to talk to
Maddox, but she wasn't sure how.

Among everything she'd considered doing—contacting her
bank and refunding him what was left of the money he'd
awarded her; going to Westville City Hall to have their marriage
annulled; hiding out in her family home for the rest of her life—
none of the options held much appeal.

It was much like the way she felt in her home. She'd held
onto it for so long because of the many cherished memories
here, because of its safety. But a home was about the people who

lived there more than anything else. Not that she didn't love Suzie, but this was completely different.

She didn't need safety. She needed the out-on-a-limb kind of bravery Maddox had encouraged her to find, that she would never have dared to seek before she'd met him.

Adelie slammed her laptop closed and rose to her feet so fast she nearly knocked it from the table. An idea struck her. It was terrifying and tempting and made her feel as though her joints had turned to jelly. But she had to.

She rushed out to the street, into her car, and drove toward the WV3 television station. It was a large rectangular structure with two massive satellite dishes on the roof. If only she'd thought to get Wendy Hendricks' contact information, but during the two encounters with the pesky news anchor, her thoughts had been too skittered to even consider it. Hopefully, she could find her now, or at least talk to someone who could help her.

A live broadcast. The idea terrified the socks off of her, but she couldn't think of any other way to prove to Maddox that she'd changed; to tell not only him but the world how she'd come to feel for him during their too-short marriage.

She'd braved a photo shoot. She'd navigated Parisienne streets alone. She'd stood up to his ex. She could do this.

The sun was a goldenrod yellow, highlighting the shrub beds speckled with spring flowers and glinting off the entrance's silver knob. Adelie reached to open it when it turned of its own accord, and Maddox stepped out.

Adelie took a staggering step backward. His appearance lit a match to her pulse, sending it sky-high. Heat flushed in her cheeks, and her vision tunneled. In his black, button-up shirt with the sleeves rolled to his forearms, his tan slacks, and tousled hair, she saw only him.

"Adelie?" he said in surprise. His hand found her elbow. The touch was a charge all its own.

"What are you doing here?" she asked.

"I could ask the same thing about you." He stepped out, letting the door close behind them. The sun glowed, presenting a halo everywhere she looked. "I was just about to head to your house because I wanted to show you something."

A metal bench sat in a collection of daffodils. Maddox accompanied Adelie to it, guiding her to sit down before taking the open space beside her. She had come to life having him close to her once more.

"Show me what?" she asked.

He pulled out his phone and tapped on a YouTube broadcast. The stage was one she recognized, the WV3 studio she'd seen on her TV screen more times than she could count. She also recognized Wendy, with her dark hair. But sitting across from her on the interview hot seat wasn't Ruby or even Duncan, as Adelie suspected it might be.

It was Maddox.

Adelie tensed in an instant. "Oh no. Maddox, what did you do?"

"Quiet, or you'll miss it," he said with a smile.

After a brief introduction, the anchor's background changed. Wendy stood in front of Wonderland's whimsical gates, but instead of gaping open in welcome to the hordes flocking in for a day of festivity, the pave stone distance from the gates to the top hat ticket booths, to the park's entrance, the spinning, coiling rides, everything was motionless, as still and silent as the morning Maddox had given her a private tour.

Wendy lifted her stout microphone to her lips and spoke.

"Wonderland is closing its doors, folks. The white rabbit is staying in hiding. Reasons behind this sudden, bold move by the park's owner, Maddox Hatter, continue to be a mystery, especially considering his recent, outlandish remodel of the attraction."

The screen returned to an image of Maddox, sitting across from Wendy in the WV3 studio. Strangely enough, in the news broadcast, he was wearing the same black, button-up shirt and tan pants he currently wore, sitting beside her.

"Did you just film this?" she asked.

He squeezed her knee. "Keep watching."

"Mr. Hatter," Wendy said, "thanks for joining me here at the studio."

"Thanks for having me," Maddox said, resting a hand on his knee. Adelie didn't fail to notice the wedding ring on his finger. Her gaze flicked to his left hand now, and butterflies coiled in her stomach at the silver band circling there.

"This news of Wonderland's sudden closure is quite the story. Would you care to share your reasons for such a drastic change?"

On the screen, Maddox shifted in his seat. His tone turned from friendly to something more sinister.

"Some rumors have begun to circulate regarding my recent marriage to Adelie Carroll, and I like to think that the truth is better than anything else, wouldn't you?"

"I would, indeed," Wendy said with a little chuckle. "All right, then, what is this truth?"

"That my personal life is no one else's business. I married Adelie Carroll because I fell in love with her, and we prefer to stay out of the public eye from now on."

"And what about Wonderland? Will you sell the park?"

"That remains to be seen," he said.

Wendy's broadcast shifted back to the image of her at Wonderland's gates. "And there you have it, folks. Looks like our billionaire is keeping things pretty close to the chest."

Wendy continued her story, giving a brief history of Wonderland along with its recent success, causing faithful attendees to marvel at this sudden and unexpected closure of such a successful park.

The video began buffering, and Maddox locked the screen with his thumb.

Adelie flurried between amazement, shock, and complete ecstasy. He'd said he loved her—on TV. He'd closed Wonderland. She wiped her clammy palms on her thighs and attempted to shake sense into her brain.

"Maddox," she breathed.

His eyes were pinned right to her. "You can search it—it's all over the internet by now. WV3 was eager for a juicy story, so when I told Wendy I had one, she hurried to get it out before anyone else."

"I—how? Why? Why would you do that?" Adelie couldn't seem to form the words. They came out in a jumbled blur.

He lowered his phone to his knee. His lips lifted into an irresistible smirk. "Do you really have to ask?"

She reached for his hand. "You can't close your park. What about your mom? Your tribute to her? And your investors—what about Duncan?"

He lifted her hand to his lips and pressed a lasting kiss to her knuckles. The touch simmered in her stomach and curled her toes in her shoes.

He spoke against her hand. "I did it because I couldn't think of any other way to tell you I love you."

Adelie's breath caught in her throat. She shifted to face him, eager for the closeness he offered.

Maddox laced his fingers with hers and put his free arm around her, drawing her to him. "I wanted to tell you I don't care about the money or the brand, but how would you ever know with the park still running as it was? You need to know, none of it matters, not if it jeopardizes you. You've come to mean more to me than I ever thought you would, I want us to stay married. I want you to continue to be my wife, Adelie."

With deliberation, Maddox shifted from the bench and knelt before her. Her heart pounded like a rabbit's hind leg. Digging in his pocket, he retrieved something and offered it in his palm. Her ring glistened in the morning sunlight.

"Adelie Hatter, will you still be my wife?" Maddox asked. "Wear my ring, take my name, and share a life with me?"

Moments like this usually landed a spotlight on her and made her feel as though a thousand eyes were watching, made her feel as though anything she said would be the wrong thing. But that dormouse was gone, hidden in a teacup. This time, Adelie sat up straight, chest fairly bursting with assurance and confidence.

"No expiration date?"

Maddox chuckled. "No end in sight. I want you forever."

She waited for a sign that this was the dream. This was the riddle, the confusing path leading only to more confusion. That any minute now she'd nibble and change size once more.

There was no shift. No confusion. No sudden change. This was reality, life outside of the rabbit hole. Maddox Hatter was kneeling before her, asking her to be his wife. Because he loved her. Because he'd gotten to know her and still wanted her.

Her response came so easily it was a wonder all of its own.

"Yes," she said, grinning from ear to ear. "Yes."

His mouth made the journey to hers with direct targeting, with deliberation and tentative slowness. The pressure was just enough. Once, twice, three times, each touch opened a new door within her, flipping on switches and creating light inside her. She mapped the way, matching his motion for motion. Resting a hand on his shoulder, his neck, weaving her fingers into his hair.

Maddox pulled away, allowing her time to absorb the sensations rippling through her. This was their land of wonder, a place only they could explore, where his touch and the gleam in his gaze belonged only to her, where she hoped he could read the devotion within her own gaze.

"I do," she said softly.

"You do what?" His hand ran up and down her spine, making her tingle.

"That's all," she said. "I do. That should have been our wedding kiss, and so I'm making my vow to you again."

Maddox's lips quirked halfway, and, still kneeling before her, he guided her to them again. "Me too," he finally said once they'd broken apart.

Even though this marriage had started out as a hoax, a cover for the protection he was offering her, it no longer was. In that moment, he was as much hers as she hoped to be his.

Wonderland was a veritable hive, buzzing and bustling with people. The streets were so tightly packed past the March Hare's house, Adelie held onto Maddox's hand just to make it through to the Red Queen's castle.

"Glad to see you two came to your senses." Duncan trudged behind, wearing a business suit with a blue shirt and tie. He continued staring at his phone, swiping through the numbers he hadn't stopped commenting on since he'd arrived a half hour before.

"I don't think Wonderland has ever had attendance like this," Maddox said, rotating and taking in the crowds. Adelie sidled next to him.

"You know, much as I hate to admit it, Ruby had it right," she said, smoothing a hand down the beading along her wedding dress—her dream dress. She and Suzie had gone to New York and met with a designer to ensure it had everything Adelie wanted. She thrilled at finally having the chance to wear it. "This really is the perfect marketing scheme for the park."

It took a lot of arguments, but several weeks later, Adelie had managed to convince her husband he should reopen. Why not use their recent marriage to the park's advantage?

She had nothing to hide, she told him. Not anymore. She was crazy in love with him and wanted to shout it on every rooftop. Adelie had never felt so happy, so completely contented, so thoroughly safe. This was home, where she belonged, and Maddox needed to know she would support him as much as he had supported her.

He loved his theme park. It meant so much to him, and she knew he'd been feeling its loss.

Finally, he'd agreed, and here they were. Adelie had convinced him to wear his tuxedo and though she'd nabbed the perfect dress, she'd had Suzie come over and help do her hair the same way it'd been done on their wedding day.

Suzie and Fletcher had taken off work. They stood near a collection of fiberglass mushrooms, chatting with Ella, Hawk, and Grammy Larsen. Adelie's chest swelled as she caught their attention. She waved in their direction as though she was some kind of princess in a parade. In this dress and with Maddox at her side, she felt like a princess.

Ella cupped her hands around her mouth and whooped. Grammy Larsen clapped, and Ella's fiancé, Hawk, waved as the surrounding crowd joined in the choral of cheers, but Suzie rushed forward and trapped Adelie in a hug.

"You deserve this," Suzie all but shouted in her ear over the noise that resulted from Ella's catcalls.

Tears stung Adelie's eyes. She squeezed her sister back just as tightly. "Your turn next."

Suzie fluttered her lips. "Yeah, right, at this rate *I'll* have to be the one who proposes." She winked at Adelie, lightening her statement, kissed her sister on the cheek, and dashed back to stand by their family. Fletcher gave Adelie a wide, toothy grin, and Adelie waved. Suzie propose? That would be a sight to witness.

Maddox wrapped an arm around her waist, tugging her close to him as they continued strolling a few more feet along the pave stone street toward the looming castle they'd agreed would be their backdrop for this. Adelie leaned her head against his chest. The space behind her ribs tripled in size and filled with so much happiness she could hardly contain it.

"I'm doing this because you wanted pictures," Maddox said, tugging his lapels.

"Of course. We need documentation." Adelie adjusted his tie, smoothing a hand over his chest. She'd never get sick of any excuse she could find to touch him. "We didn't take a single one on our wedding day, and I'm remedying that. I want to hang them all over the house."

Maddox gave an acquiescent smile. He stood as though he felt out of place. "At least Duncan will be happy."

"I'm not doing this for Duncan." Adelie glanced to where Duncan stood, in conversation with Ritchie, who'd bent over to retrieve the camera from its case.

"No, but we should. He's been a good sport about continuing to remain an investor, even with my ups and downs the past few weeks."

That he had. Duncan had been Maddox's most severe worry. He'd let his friend down by pulling the rug out from under him the way he had. Duncan had given Maddox a chance, and it'd been eating away at Maddox that he hadn't done right by him.

Adelie put her arms around him. "I'm glad you decided to reopen."

"So am I. I'm glad people are actually coming," he muttered, squinting around.

Ritchie approached, his camera in hand, black fingernail

already on the button. He took his photographer stance and tilted the camera at an angle before his face.

"Don't move. The light here is perfect."

He snapped a few pictures, aiming the camera first horizontal, then vertical. "We should get one of you both here, in the middle of the croquet grounds."

Between a pair of arborvitaes, he directed them where to stand. "No need for you to look lost this time, eh?" Ritchie said as a joke.

Adelie's smile overtook her. The accompanying joy was too much to contain. No, she wasn't hiding anything anymore. She knew exactly where she wanted to be, and who she wanted to be with. Thanks to a wild goose chase—or rather, a rabbit chase—she'd found her life, and she never wanted to leave it or Maddox again.

Maddox's arms encircled her, and she ducked her head against his chest at the catcalls and whistles from onlookers.

"Are you happy, Mrs. Hatter?" he asked.

"More than I've ever been."

"Even with all these people watching you?"

She tugged him closer, tiptoeing up for another kiss. "Let them look. As long as I have you, I can handle anything."

Duncan fiddled with the top button of his dress shirt and nearly tore the thing off before it relented and came loose. Frustration was usually his go-to these days, but he was in Wonderland, overseeing Maddox and Adelie's wedding photo shoot. Things were back in motion, and Wonderland's attendance was higher than it had been to date. Which meant his investment would pan out, just as he'd known it would from the start of this whole charade with Adelie.

Why then was he so flat out irritated?

His assistant, Rosabel, sauntered toward him, killing it in dark slacks, a blue, button-up shirt with no collar. Those heels, though. She should know what they did when she walked.

Full lips darker than rubies, she smirked at Duncan and stopped at his side. Her dark hair shined in the sunlight. Duncan stuffed his hands in his pockets to keep from reaching out to touch it.

"What are you doing here?" he asked her, not caring that his tone had all the friendliness of a shark.

"Maddox invited me," she said.

"That's what I get for trying to be nice," he grumbled, cursing himself for letting Maddox get to know her.

"What do you care whether I'm here or not?"

"I don't," Duncan lied. He still couldn't figure out what had his temper so on edge. He'd only ever invested in what he considered worth his while, and once Maddox had gotten Adelie Carroll to pose as Alice, Wonderland was culminating as one of the best investments Duncan had made.

Then Maddox had to go and get his heart caught in the mix, pulling everything out from under Duncan. It was a low blow, to say the least. Still, his company would recover, thanks to the closure being so short-lived. As for his friendship, well...

All right. That would recover too. He and Maddox had been friends too long for it not to.

But to do something so stupid for love? To throw his entire business on the line just to prove something to a woman? Duncan prayed he was never that idiotic.

Was that what bothered him? That Maddox had gone and fallen in love with the girl?

He peered at Rosabel. She was a knockout no matter what she wore, that was for sure, from her pointed gaze to her feathery eye lashes, to the sharp remarks she managed to throw back at him. She was exciting in a world of the ordinary.

People at the office already thought they were into each other, which was one reason Duncan couldn't —absolutely refused to—admit he was falling for her.

Besides, it was also obvious that Rosabel couldn't stand him.

Regardless of all that, what did it matter that Maddox had fallen in love? He didn't care. Duncan didn't mind in the slightest that even though his friend had found happiness with a woman, he never could.

In the distance, Maddox gathered Adelie into his arms. Her white, flowing dress trailed the pave stones, and the crowd around them erupted into cheers as he dipped in for a kiss with their photographer capturing every second of it.

Good grief, this was ridiculous. Duncan had to get over himself.

Still, something streaked through him as, beaming, Rosabel joined in the applause.

"Aren't you glad I helped them out?" Duncan taunted from behind her.

She glanced back, her eyes flashing. "Don't do that."

"Do what?"

Rosabel slanted herself toward him, turning away from the happy couple. "I know you're taking credit for this fantastic moment for them, but news flash, Duncan Hawthorne, you are not the reason those two got together."

"I was the one who got you to help with their wedding and their honeymoon."

"Which I did gladly." She punched his arm. "Now stop arguing with me. You're ruining a perfect day."

Duncan sniggered, and at that moment, with her playful, almost flirtatious arm-punch, a thought struck him.

What if a relationship with Rosabel wasn't impossible?

He refused to believe Rosabel felt nothing for him, or that this animosity of hers was genuine. He'd tried suppressing his interest in her...but what if he stopped?

So what if she was his assistant? Maddox Hatter wasn't the only one who could pull a fast-one on an unsuspecting recipient. After capturing another quick glance of Maddox kissing Adelie in front of the Ferris wheel, the realization sank hard into Duncan's sternum, hammering itself in with the force of a fence post digger.

As far as Duncan saw things, he had two options.

He could put his feelings for Rosabel to rest once and for all. Continue simmering in this frustration or just fire her and do his best to forget her.

Or he could let Rosabel know how he felt. He could see where things might lead.

The prospect of that, he admitted to himself, was tempting and terrifying all at once.

Thanks for reading! Continue on for a sneak peek of *Rosabel and the Billionaire Beast!*

ROSABEL AND THE BILLIONAIRE BEAST SNEAK PEEK

Soon enough, the handle turned, and there she was. Instead of standing in the doorway, Rosabel entered his office and closed the door. She was exasperated, as usual, looking just as tired as she had earlier. Her hair draped in chestnut waves past her shoulders, and she smoothed a hand over her pencil skirt.

"Do you even hear the way you talk to me?" she said, without asking what he wanted as she usually did. "I should quit."

This was new. She'd never talked about quitting before. Amusing, considering how he'd recently—jokingly—contemplated firing her. He moved in closer, momentarily forgetting what he'd called her in here for. "Okay, then. Why don't you?"

"What?"

"You heard me. Why don't you quit?"

Rosabel's mouth parted. She really needed to stop wearing that lip gloss.

Thoughts fled, unable to follow a direct course with her standing so near. He could tell something troubled her. She was tired, that much was obvious, but a different kind of weariness settled over her. He wanted to ask what the problem was, but he already did once this morning. Doing so again would destroy the careful nothing he'd kept between them thus far.

"I need the job."

Duncan tucked two fingers into his pocket. "You're a strong, talented, efficient woman. You could find work in any number of places. So why don't you?"

The most delicious shade of pink filled her cheeks. She didn't dip her chin or show any other sign of flattery that could put him at ease or give an inclination that she was affected by him. Instead, she pegged her gaze right to him as mysterious confusion crossed over her face. "You paid me a compliment," she said.

"What?"

"You just said something nice about me. Right to my face."

This time, Duncan's cheeks heated. The rumors were already thick enough. He didn't need to go adding to them by complimenting her. "You're avoiding my question."

She inched another step closer. "You're avoiding the fact that you said something nice about me."

"Pfft." He fluttered his lips and stalked back, needing to space to think. "I say all kinds of nice things about you."

Rosabel folded her arms. "Sure you do."

"I do. You're just never around to hear it."

Her eyes softened in a way they never had before, revealing the vulnerability he'd sensed the minute she'd stepped in. What was going on? Typically, she was all claws-out, ready to spring. "Why not?" Her voice was deathly soft.

"What?"

"Why don't you ever tell me nice things?"

Duncan cleared his throat. "I don't know." He hurried to think of something to douse the heat in her gaze. "Look. I'm heading out of town and ..." Now or never. For some reason, he couldn't bring himself to ask her. "And ... I need you to pick up my dry cleaning. I have to start packing."

"Dry cleaning?" Her jaw quivered, and the sight of tears welling in her eyes took him aback. "If you had any idea what I just—" She slammed her eyes closed, holding a hand to stop him as though he were in the process of advancing toward her. Rosabel drew in a slow breath and gradually lifted her long lashes. Her jaw was set. Her eyes were fire. He couldn't figure out why this set her off. Picking up his dry cleaning was a regular thing. "Fine. You want me to quit? I quit."

"What?"

Rosabel stormed from his office without answering, her hips swaying, her heels clacking on the floor.

Duncan felt as though a brick struck him. She wasn't supposed to accept. She was supposed to quip back the way they always did. Against his better judgment, he called after her, too loud to be inconspicuous. "Rosabel, wait!"

She spun, nostrils flaring. Gopher heads popped over the tops of cubicles once more. Duncan's ears flamed. Usually, their nosiness didn't bother him—he could snap and crackle, and they would pop right back to what they were doing before. This was different somehow. He got the feeling he'd hurt Rosabel, and he wasn't sure what to do about it.

"Don't go yet," he said, shifting his gaze around at the eavesdroppers. "Come back in my office. We can talk there."

"No."

"Yes."

Her jaw clenched. Too late, he realized he had reached for her. Rosabel shook him off. He'd never manhandled a woman that way before—never mind what people thought of him.

Her shifting gaze told him she felt the weight of their avid audience.

"Don't you all have work to do?" Duncan snapped toward the onlookers.

Rosabel jutted her chin, fury raging in her expression. "I'll come, but because *I* want to. Not because you're demanding it of me." She brushed past him, sweeping her perfume in his direction.

Duncan trudged after her, cursing the onlooking eyes. If there weren't rumors about him and Rosabel before, there certainly would be now. He slammed his office door for good measure.

"What was that about?" he snarled. "You can't just up and quit."

She pierced him with a glower.

"Come on, Rosie. I can tell something is bothering you. What's going on?"

"My father has Alzheimer's."

Duncan's mouth dropped. Serious conversations weren't what he was after, but he couldn't dismiss this. Rosabel had never been open with him about anything personal before. If he was being honest with himself, he hadn't ever really considered her personal life. She was only someone who was fun to argue with.

But Alzheimer's? No wonder she appeared to be hanging on by a thread.

"He has Alzheimer's," she repeated, brow pinched and tears seeping down her cheeks. "He needs constant care, and I can't be there for him if I'm here working for you, the Jerky Beast Boss who can't be bothered to compliment me to my face. Do you have any idea how much I do for you, and you can't even say 'thank you'?" Her voice climbed in pitch.

Duncan gestured to the chair in front of his desk. "Maybe you should sit down."

"I don't want to."

He lifted his hands. "Okay, then. Quit. See how well you'll care for your dad when you're too broke to feed yourself."

"You have some nerve."

"Just putting things into perspective for you."

She bared her teeth. "Believe me, I have plenty of perspective. I'm stuck. I'm totally stuck. You clearly take me for granted. So give me one good reason why I should stay."

"Because I need you—"

Eyes wide, she lifted her chin.

He thought quickly, hurrying to remedy what had almost sounded like some kind of romantic admission. "I need you to come to Arkansas with me."

He wanted some way to smooth things over with his family. Maybe if they met and liked Rosabel, their approval could iron out his family's years-long mix-up. He'd been in a sort of battle-of-the-sexes association with Rosabel since she'd started working for him. That was a relationship all on its own, wasn't it? The only unknown was Rosabel. His family would never accept that he was dating his assistant. Would she consider a change to their relationship? Taking things between them up a step?

Duncan blamed Maddox. If his best friend's fake relationship with his model hadn't turned out so amazingly, Duncan would never have given this a second thought. But a fake relationship might be what both he and Rosabel needed.

Duncan strolled to the window and parted the blinds with two fingers. The street below was noisy with cars and traffic— which, for a small town like Westville, Vermont, was saying something. "My grandmother is turning ninety-five." He spoke with his back to her, knowing innately that she was still there, still listening.

"Congratulations." She didn't sound like she meant it.

Duncan smirked and faced her. "I've been invited home to celebrate her birthday, but I'd prefer not to go alone."

"What does that mean?"

"I want them to think I'm seeing someone."

"Aren't you?"

If he was, she would know. She knew his schedule better than he did.

Duncan scraped a hand behind his neck. "Yeah. You."

Rosabel shook her head. "You're so full of yourself."

"I may have mentioned I'd bring someone to the party, and since I didn't tell her who, my mother may have misconstrued the nature of our relationship."

"Your mom thinks we're dating too? Is there anyone who doesn't?" Rosabel folded her arms. "What exactly have you been saying about me to give her that impression?"

"Nothing," he said, too defensively. "You just come into my mind more than I realize, I guess, so when she asked, I assumed you'd come."

"And why is that?"

"Because I'm stuck being around you all the time."

Her almond eyes thinned to slits. "If you're about to ask something of me, you're not off to a great start."

"I'm just saying, well, enough people think we're dating. Why don't we?"

Rosabel closed her eyes and pinched the bridge of her nose. At least she'd stopped crying. "You want to date me?"

"Why not? Everyone already thinks we are anyway." He threw a hand toward the closed door currently facilitating the gossip that undoubtedly circled the cubicles that moment.

Her lips pinched tighter. She placed her hands on her hips as though ready to rip into him.

Duncan hurried to convince her before she could. "Come home with me to Arkansas. Let me introduce you to my family and placate my grandmother at what could be her last birthday." The final comment as a little low, even for him. He rolled with it.

Rosabel didn't miss a beat. She lifted her chin. "Slather on a dose of manipulation, why don't you?"

He lifted his hands in mock surrender. "I'm not manipulating you." Who was he kidding? He was totally manipulating her.

"No?"

"It was—" He released an irritated sigh. He didn't usually have to work this hard to secure new clients or contracts. "Not a guilt trip."

"No." Rosabel's tone was flat.

"What?"

She took a step forward. "No, I don't want to date you. It's hard enough working for you and having to deal with your problems and demands. I think a relationship would ruin any kind of professional interaction we have if we were to involve closer knowledge of each other."

Duncan's lips quirked upward. He couldn't help it. "Who said we would be close?"

Rosabel fidgeted. "Dating implies something like that." She was blushing? Good. "Especially if we're going to convince your family there's more than animosity between us."

This grew more interesting by the minute. "Is there more than animosity between us?"

She reduced her eyes into dagger slits. "What do you think?"

This time Duncan took a step forward, his voice sinking to a captivating pitch. "I think I wouldn't mind finding out."

Read Rosabel and Duncan's story in *Rosabel and the Billionaire Beast!*

Copyright © 2020 Cortney Pearson
All rights reserved.
No part of this publication may be reproduced, stored in or
introduced into a retrieval system or transmitted, in any form or
by any means—electronic, mechanical, printing, recording, or
otherwise—without the prior permission of the author, except
for use of brief quotations in a book review.

This book is a work of fiction. Names, characters, organizations,
places, incidents, or events are either products of the author's
imagination or are used fictitiously. Any resemblance to actual
events, locales or persons, living or dead, is entirely coincidental.

Beta Read by Scarlett West
Copy Edited/Proofread by Sara Olds with Salt & Sage Books
Cover Design by Najla Qamber Designs
Interior Formatting by Nada Qamber
Author Photo by Clayton Photo + Design

www.catelynmeadows.com

Made in the USA
Columbia, SC
09 June 2023

17768359R00143